# rash

# Also by Pete Hautman

# PETE HAUTMAN

# rash

Simon Pulse

New York    London    Toronto    Sydney

ᗢ

SIMON PULSE
An imprint of Simon & Schuster Children's Publishing Division
1230 Avenue of the Americas, New York, NY 10020
Copyright © 2006 by Pete Hautman
All rights reserved, including the right of reproduction in
whole or in part in any form.
SIMON PULSE and colophon are registered trademarks
of Simon & Schuster, Inc.
Also available in a Simon & Schuster Books for
Young Readers hardcover edition.
Designed by Jessica Sonkin
The text of this book was set in Melior.
Manufactured in the United States of America
First Simon Pulse edition December 2007
8  10  9  7
The Library of Congress has cataloged the hardcover edition
as follows:
Hautman, Pete, 1952–
Rash / Pete Hautman.—1st ed.
p. cm.
Summary: In a future society that has decided it would "rather be
safe than be free," sixteen-year-old Bo's anger control problems land
him in a tundra jail where he survives with the help of his running
skills and an artificial intelligence program named Bork.
[1. Self-control—Fiction. 2. Individuality—Fiction. 3. Football—
Fiction. 4. Artificial intelligence—Fiction.] I. Title.
ISBN-13: 978-0-689-86801-6 (hc)
ISBN-10: 0-689-86801-4 (hc)
Pz7.H2887Ras  2006
[Fic]—dc222005015251
ISBN-13: 978-0-689-86904-4  (pbk)
ISBN-10: 0-689-86904-5  (pbk)

For Tyler

I pledge Allegiance
to the Flag
of the Safer States of America
and to the Republic
for which it stands
one Nation
under Law
with Security
and Safety
for All.

# PART ONE
## the droog

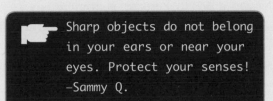

☞ Sharp objects do not belong
in your ears or near your
eyes. Protect your senses!
—Sammy Q.

Gramps, who was born in 1990, once told
me that when he was my age the only way to wind up in
prison in the USSA (back when it had only one S) was to
steal something, kill somebody, or use illegal drugs.

"Illegal drugs? You mean like beer?" I asked, pointing
at his mug of home brew.

He laughed. "No, Bo. Beer was legal back then. I'm talking about heroin, marijuana, and cocaine. Drugs like that."

"They sent people to *jail* for that?"

"They sure did," he said, sipping his beer. Gramps's
home brewed beer was one of our family secrets.

"Why didn't they just regenerate their dopamine
receptors?"

"They didn't have the technology back then, Bo. It was
a different world."

"Yeah, but sending them to a work camp . . . that sounds kind of extreme."

"No more extreme than putting a person away for littering," Gramps said.

"Littering is only a class-four misdemeanor—you don't get sent up for that."

"Mr. Stoltz did."

"That was for assault. Melody Haynes got hurt."

"But all he did, really, was litter. He dropped an apricot when he was unloading groceries from his suv."

"Yeah, then Melody slipped on it and got a concussion."

"She should have been wearing her helmet. My point is, Bo, all the man did was drop an apricot and they sent him away for a whole year. A year of hard labor on a prison farm. For dropping an apricot!"

"But if he hadn't dropped it, Melody wouldn't have gotten bonked," I said. Sometimes my grandfather could be kind of dense.

"Maybe so, Bo," he said, "but the fact remains, the poor man lost a whole year of his life for one lousy apricot."

Gramps could get real stubborn when he'd been drinking.

Back then there were five of us Marstens serving time: my father, my brother, two cousins, and an aunt.

My dad got put away for roadrage back in '73. Some droog pulled out in front of him, and Dad caught up with him at the next traffic light and jumped out of his car and pounded his fist on the hood of the guy's suv and made an obscene gesture. It would have been no big deal except that it was his third roadrage citation, so he was sentenced to five years under the three-strikes-you're-out law.

Last year my brother Sam went to an unauthorized graduation party and got in a fistfight. The kid he fought lost a tooth. Sam was seventeen at the time.

Like father, like son—they sentenced Sam to two years. If he'd been an adult, he would've gotten five years, minimum.

I never found out why my aunt and cousins were locked up. Most people don't like to talk about their jailed family members. It's embarrassing. But having five close relatives in the prison system is not that unusual. According to *USSA Today,* 24 percent of all adults in this country are serving time. My family was only slightly more criminal than average.

Dad got sent to a prison aquafarm down in Louisiana. He wrote to us that by the time he is released, he will have shelled twenty million shrimp. That message included a thirty-second clip of him standing at his workstation, blue gloves up to his elbows, ripping into a bin of crustaceans. Sam was on a road gang in Nebraska, middle of nowhere, patching holes on the interstate.

Of course, without people like us Marstens, there wouldn't be anybody to do the manual labor that makes this country run. Without penal workers, who would work the production lines, or pick the melons and peaches, or maintain the streets and parks and public lavatories? Our economy depends on prison labor. Without it everybody would have to work—whether they wanted to or not.

Anyway, here's my point: Given my family's history I should have known to keep an eye on my temper. Lose control for one tiny chunk of time and *bam*—next thing you know you're ripping the legs off shrimp. But at the time . . . Well, if you look at history, you will see that I was not the first guy to do something really stupid over a girl. Look at how many Greeks died for Helen of Troy. How much self-control do you think they had?

# 2

I was never very good at school things. Historical events didn't stick in my head. Science and math bored me. As for dealing with people, forget about it. I could never have been a counselor, or a doctor, or a politician. I didn't have the patience.

I was no better at the arts: Painting, sculpture, and music didn't do it for me. Not that anybody else was any good at those things. All the best art got made back in the last millennium, before we learned how to fix depression and schizophrenia and stuff. These days, with everybody more or less sane, the new art is about as interesting as oatmeal.

According to my sixteenth-year Career Indexing Evaluation, my top career choice was correctional worker. I guess that meant I'd make a good prison guard. Or maybe a good prisoner. Either way, with penal institutions being such big business I'd have no problem finding work if I wanted it.

The only thing I'd ever been really good at was running. I could run faster than anyone else on Washington Campus, with the possible exception of the intolerable

Karlohs Mink. I could run a 50-yard dash in eight seconds, and 100 meters in under 14 seconds.

In fact, on the day I got into it with Karlohs Mink, I had been hoping to break the 100-meter school record of 13.33 seconds.

Karlohs was never my favorite person. Even before the first time he looked at Maddy Wilson, I hadn't liked him. For one thing, the way he spelled his first name was really irritating. And I hated his wrinkly minky smirk. And his stupid-looking asymmetrical hair: so pretentious; so 2060s. The only thing I liked about Karlohs was his last name. *Mink.* It was perfect that he had the name of a diminutive, beady-eyed, nasty-smelling member of the weasel family.

But I never set out to harm his smirking minky face. At least not at first. Not until he started his minky sniffing around Maddy Wilson.

I had called Maddy that morning and told her I was about to set a new school record for the 100 meter.

"Oh, Bo," she said, her laughing face filling my WindO, "you are so funny."

I don't know why Maddy did it for me. Something about her mouth and eyes lit me up every time I saw her. I wanted desperately to impress her.

"I'm serious, Mad. I'm gonna set a new school record."

"I think you and Karlohs are simply ridiculous."

"Karlohs? What's he got to do with it?"

"You're both just so *competitive.*"

"Maybe so. But I got the bear after me."

"Oh, Bo, you and your silly bear!"

· · ·

Back when Gramps was in high school, kids ran faster. Gramps claimed to have run 100 meters in 11 seconds, and the mile in 4:37. That was before the Child Safety Act of 2033. Now every high school runner has to wear a full set of protective gear—AtherSafe shoes with lateral ankle support and four layers of memory gel in the thick soles, knee pads, elbow pads, neck brace, tooth guard, wrist monitor, and an FDHHSS-certified sports helmet. We raced on an Adzorbium® track with its five centimeters of compacted gel-foam topped by a thick sheet of artificial latex. It's like running on a sponge.

Before the Child Safety Act dozens of high school athletes died in accidents every year. They died from things like heatstroke, skull fractures, heart attacks, and broken necks. Today, high school athletes are as safe on the athletic field as they are sitting in the classroom.

Gramps thought it was ridiculous.

"They might just as well put you in a rubber room and see who can stomp their feet up and down the fastest," he once said. "We used to run on hard-packed cinders—no helmets, no gel-foam, none a that."

I tried to argue: "But, Gramps, it's just as healthy. I mean, with the equipment and the Adzorbium, we probably get twice the workout, only nobody gets bonked."

"Nobody goes very fast, either. I ever show you my old track shoes?"

"Yes, Gramps. I've seen them." Gramps kept his old running shoes in a box in the garage. Every now and then he'd bring them out and wave them around and go on and on about the days of the "real" athletes. You couldn't talk to him when he got like that.

"Look, Gramps, as long as we all have the same rules, the top athlete still gets the trophy."

"That why you run, Bo? For trophies? Hell, when I was a boy, reason we ran was 'cause we were getting chased. We played *football* back then. *Real* football. *Tackle* football."

Football has been illegal since before I was born. I've seen recordings of the old games, and I can see why it has been banned. The only place they play it now is in some South American countries like Columbistan and Paraguay.

"It was run like the devil or get eaten up." Gramps had drunk a few beers that day.

"Yeah, right. Who'd want to eat you?"

"You'd be surprised, boy. It was the twentieth century back then. Bears everywhere."

"You were chased by bears?"

"Damn straight, boy."

"You don't expect me to believe that, do you?"

"Hell, boy, some of the things you kids believe these days . . . how do I know *what* you'll believe? But I'll tell you this: You want to run a little faster? Just imagine you got a grizzly on your ass."

Coach Hackenshor thought I had a future as a distance runner, but of course that would have to wait until I graduated. For safety reasons, the school bans running distances greater than 1000 meters.

The day I got into it with Karlohs Mink we were running time trials in preparation for our track meet with Graves Academy. I was feeling particularly fast and strong that morning. As I changed into my running gear, I imagined myself flying across the track, shoes digging into the spongy Adzorbium surface, arms pumping, wind whistling through the vents in my helmet. As I strapped on my knee guards, I imagined my legs like pistons, each stride propelling me effortlessly to unheard-of speeds. I imagined Karlohs Mink in my wake, red-faced and gasping.

Thirteen seconds is a long time to run flat out. Most runners hold back a little at first, not reaching their top speed until they cover half the distance. I preferred Gramps's technique: Run like you got a grizzly on your ass.

Four of us were suited up and ready to run: Me, Matt Gelman, Ron White, and Karlohs Mink. We were milling around the starting blocks waiting for Hackenshor to tell us to take our positions for the first time trial. It was only ten a.m., but already getting hot. The Adzorbium had a gluey, sticky feel, and I was starting to sweat. My knees were feeling scratchy, and I realized that I'd forgotten to put on my kneepad liners. No time now, even though the pad liners were required gear. They're supposed to prevent chafing. But I only had to run 100 meters. Hackenshor would never notice. I looked at my wrist monitor. Heartbeat 62 beats per minute. Body temperature 98.4° F. Air temperature 78° F. If it got much hotter, they'd call off the trials. Not a great day for setting new school records, but I was going to give it my best shot. I had even skipped my morning dose of Levulor®.

I had been taking Levulor ever since I was twelve. Three fourths of the students at Washington took the stuff. Basically, if you have a temper tantrum after the age of ten, they put you on it. Levulor works by delaying the anger reflex—you get an extra tenth of a second to think before you act. But it seemed to slow down all the reflexes, even the good ones, so I usually skipped my morning dose when we had track meets and time trials.

Karlohs Mink, who liked to boast that he did not need Levulor, was my only serious competition in the 100 meter. He had the advantage of longer legs, greater speed, and superior endurance, and he knew it. But there was one thing Karlohs lacked.

He did not have a grizzly bear on his ass.

"Hey, Marsten," he said to me, "I hear you're planning to set a new record today."

That took me by surprise. "Where'd you hear that?"

"Maddy told me," he said, smirking in that phony friendly way.

Maddy? Why had he been talking to Maddy? More to the point, why had Maddy told him anything about me?

"I'm just gonna do my best," I said, shrugging it off. On the outside I was cucumber cool, but inside I was starting to boil. I knew he was trying to get under my skin. Maddy Wilson was *my* girlfriend. Just having her and Karlohs in the same thought set my teeth on edge.

"She said you pretend a bear is chasing you when you run," Karlohs said, his smile growing larger.

"I don't know what you're talking about," I said, returning his smile. But inside I was screaming. *Maddy! What were you thinking? How could you tell Karlohs Mink the things I say for your ears alone?* Sure, I'd told Maddy about my grizzly-bear technique. And I'd bragged to her that I might set a new school record. But why did she have to share it with Karlohs?

Matt and Ron were listening.

"What bear?" Matt asked.

Karlohs said, "He pretends a bear is chasing him."

"No, I don't," I said.

"Does it help?" Ron asked.

"There is no bear."

Hackenshor blew his whistle and we all took our positions on the blocks. I was sick with suppressed anger. My knees felt shaky and my running gear weighed a thousand pounds. Karlohs had his smirky grin turned on me. Hackenshor was shouting, and suddenly, before I was ready, came the loud crack of the starter pistol. Karlohs was out of the blocks before the signal got to my legs—then I was running, Adzorbium sucking at my soles, and all I could think of was that I was behind, Karlohs Mink's bright-blue-on-yellow number 19 singlet a body length in front of me. My arms were pumping, elbow pads, kneepads, and ankle braces clattering. My legs were made of lead. Too late I remembered the grizzly bear on my ass, but it had lost its power. Karlohs had killed the bear. Instead of catching up and blowing past the competition, I watched as the gap between us widened.

I finished dead last, my time an embarrassing 14.39 seconds.

After the race, Karlohs came over and offered me his hand.

"Good race," he said.

"Listen, Mink," I said, unfastening my helmet, "I want you to stay away from Maddy." I pulled off my helmet.

His eyes opened wide in mock astonishment. "Excuse me? I don't believe I need your permission to talk to anyone."

"Just stay away from her."

Karlohs removed his own helmet so I could see his entire smirky face, and he laughed. That was what did it.

I threw my helmet on the ground.

"She doesn't want anything to do with a pretentious droog like you," I said, getting right in his face. "So leave her alone, okay? I don't want your disgusting dog-anus mouth anywhere near her, understand?"

Karlohs staggered back as if he had been struck. I felt a moment of satisfaction followed immediately by a sick feeling. I knew I'd gone too far, even though it was true—

his mouth really did look like the south end of a beagle. But verbally attacking someone's physical appearance is a class-three misdemeanor.

Then I watched as Karlohs's eyes went glittery and his anus lips spread across his face in a smile. I picked up my helmet, turned, and walked away with a lead weight in my belly and a prickling on the back of my neck. I already had two violations on my record.

Three strikes and you're out.

# 4

I hoped that my little tiff with Karlohs would be overlooked. I'm sure it was recorded by one of the security sensors on the athletic field, but Security, Safety, and Health couldn't monitor every moment of every day.

Still, I was plenty worried.

Last winter I had gotten in trouble for throwing a pencil during Ms. Hildebrand's art class. We were drawing a bowl of fruit. People have been drawing fruit for hundreds of years. I don't know why they don't just use an imager.

Anyway, I happened to look at Matt Gelman two rows over, and I noticed he'd broken the tip off his pencil. I had an extra one, so I caught his eye and tossed it over to him. It was not a good throw. The pencil flew over Matt and embedded itself point-first in Ty Green's forehead. Ty let out a howl, Ms. Hildebrand went ballistic, and I ended up in a world of trouble. Nobody believed it was an accident. I was charged with a class-two misdemeanor, put on probation for a month, and graphite pencils were banned from the school.

Strike one.

A few months later I was late for track practice. I ran down the hall toward the locker room. Running in school is against safety regs, of course, but the hall was almost empty and I was in a hurry. Then this stupid droog of a senior grabbed me and said to slow down. I don't know what got into me, but I told him to mind his own damn business. Oh, and I shoved him against the wall. He got a little bump on the back of his head, and I got suspended for a week.

Strike two.

I blame it all on my father. Other kids could just breeze through school with never a problem. They weren't cursed with those Marsten genes. My father should have known that his children would be doomed to end up in prison. He knew he had a temper. Some people shouldn't breed, my father being a prime example.

Maybe when he decided to have kids, he didn't know he'd end up in prison, but that doesn't make it any less his fault. I wished he wasn't so much a part of me.

I showered and went to Ms. Martinez's USSA history class, where we were studying the 2030s—as boring a decade as can be imagined. I tried to make myself believe that nothing would happen. If Karlohs didn't rat me out, I thought I might be okay.

It's not quite true that the 2030s were the most boring decade of all time. The 2070s were even more tedious. We haven't had a war or a major natural disaster since 2059, the year before I was born. That was when the

17

Christian Fundamentalist Crusade flew a remote control bomb-copter into the Lincoln Memorial, leveling it with a single blast. The Bible, the CFC terrorists claimed, forbade the worship of graven images. That was the last interesting thing that happened in the USSA, as far as I'm concerned.

Ms. Martinez started out by telling us about the gun riots of 2039, which sound a lot more interesting than they were. It wasn't as if people were out on the streets shooting at each other—the gun riots took place in c-space. An extremist gun collectors' group called the NRA launched a spam attack on the web that jammed servers on every continent. But instead of getting their message across, the extremists only managed to outrage the entire human race. Local police departments were deluged with calls from angry citizens ratting out their gun-hoarding neighbors, which soon led to the nation-wide confiscation of all firearms. If the police ever found out that Gramps had a shotgun hidden under his bed, he'd spend the rest of his life on a high security workfarm.

I drifted off, imagining what it was like back in the days when people owned guns and shot one another all the time. How angry would you have to be to shoot somebody?

Even Karlohs Mink didn't deserve that.

"Bo," said Ms. Martinez.

I blinked and sat up straight.

"Pop quiz, Bo."

Everybody was bent over their WindOs. I opened mine and read the first question:

1. The expression "One hundred healthy
years for every man, woman, and child"
led Congress to pass what act on
September 13, 2033?

That was an easy one. I typed in the answer:

The Child Safety Act.

The next question was harder.

2. Which of the following crimes were
legal prior to 2023?
a. alcohol consumption
b. private ownership of large dogs
c. hunting
d. public defecation
e. driving without a safety web
f. boxing
g. chain saw possession

I had no idea. Every one of the crimes listed struck
me as outrageous. It had to be a trick question. I
answered:

None of the above.

Next question:

3. In what year did President Denton
Wilke sign into law a bill outlawing

body piercing, tattooing, branding, and
other forms of self-mutilation?

I didn't know that one either, but since we were
studying the 2030s, I had a one-in-ten chance of getting
it right. I was about to guess 2035 when my WindO went
dark, then lit up with the words:

PLEASE REPORT IMMEDIATELY TO
MR. LIPKIN AT SECURITY,
SAFETY, AND HEALTH.

# 5

Mr. Lipkin was strapped in his survival chair and plugged into a multiset. I sat down on the low padded bench that ran across the back wall of his office and waited for him to notice me. Sometimes it took a while. The multiset connected him to sensors in every room, hallway, closet, and office in the school. I think it was hard for him to disengage. I made myself comfortable and began working on my defense.

At Washington Campus, verbal attacks are taken very seriously. It wouldn't help my case to claim that I had been unduly provoked. No matter what Karlohs had done or said to me, my attack on him was a class-three misdemeanor. My only hope was to convince Lipkin that I had been making an ironic joke when I called Karlohs a "pretentious droog." I would still be punished for hurting Karlohs's feelings, but as long as I could prove it wasn't malicious, it might not qualify as a misdemeanor. As for the dog-anus comment, maybe I could say I thought dog asses were beautiful. I didn't expect him to buy it, but it was worth a try. Maybe I'd get off with a warning.

After making me wait a few minutes, Lipkin unplugged

the multiset from the socket in his temple and placed it in a compartment on the side of his chair. The chair was a Roland Survivor, top of the line. Only a few of the school faculty—those who were born rich or who had won a large lawsuit—could afford survival chairs. Originally designed for people with serious heart conditions, the chairs had become a fad recently among those who could heft the V$5,000,000-plus price tag. I guess if you have the money it makes sense, in a way. According to the manufacturer, a Roland Survivor will extend the life of its owner by an average of seventeen months. That's assuming that you keep your butt planted in the chair twenty-four hours a day.

Lipkin touched a pad on the arm. The chair rotated a few degrees to face me, then rose up on its wheels, raising Lipkin's head to standing height so that I had to tip my head back to look at his wobbly chins.

"Bo Marsten," he said in his reedy voice. "You have once again failed to control your antisocial impulses."

"I am sorry," I said.

"We have recorded five violations. Would you like me to read them to you?"

"That isn't necessary," I said. "I know I was out of line, sir."

"Out of line? I think your actions were somewhat more serious than that, Bo."

He waited a few seconds to give me a chance to respond, but I kept my mouth shut for once.

"First," Lipkin said, reading from the WindO attached to the left arm of his survival chair, "you called Karlohs Mink a 'pretentious droog.' Do you know what a droog is, Bo?"

"Not really."

"It was originally derived from a Russian word meaning 'friend,' but in modern slang usage it means something like 'worthless fool.' It is a word favored by the lower classes—criminals, incompetents, morons, and reactionaries. It is not an expression we are accustomed to hearing uttered here on Washington Campus. Do you not agree?"

"I guess."

"How would you feel if someone called you a pretentious, worthless fool?"

"I guess I wouldn't like it much."

"In fact, your calling Mr. Mink a pretentious droog was a verbal assault with intent to inflict emotional trauma, was it not?"

"I was just kidding around. I didn't mean to bonk him."

"Second violation: You unfavorably and maliciously compared Mr. Mink's mouth to an unsavory part of a dog's anatomy."

"Technically, that's true," I said. "You see, I noticed that when he wrinkled his mouth up the way he does, it looked sort of like a dog's . . . um . . . rear end. I didn't mean anything bad by it; I just happened to notice the resemblance."

"Verbal assault, count two," said Lipkin, touching the screen of his WindO. "Which brings me to your third violation. Have you been taking your Levulor, Bo?"

"Um, yes. . . ."

"Do I need to order a saliva test?"

"I might've forgot this morning."

"Skipping your Levulor dose is a violation of school policy, Bo."

"I know." There is no defense for violating a medication

order, but usually skipping a day or two isn't taken seriously. Kids forget sometimes.

"Take your Levulor, Bo."

"Now?"

"Now."

"Yes, sir." I unclipped my medipack from my belt, slid a blue tab from the dispenser, and placed it under my tongue. It dissolved instantly.

Lipkin nodded, then said, "Number four. You were not wearing proper protection during this afternoon's track-and-field practice."

"Oh." I didn't think they would notice the missing knee-pad liners. Those surveillance cameras must be better than I thought. "I got dressed in a hurry."

"That is no excuse."

"I know," I said.

Lipkin stared glumly at his WindO, shaking his head slowly. "Finally, we have attempted destruction of school property."

"We do?" That surprised me.

"You threw your helmet on the ground."

"Wait a second. Those helmets are supposed to be unbreakable. I wasn't trying to destroy it, I just dropped it!"

"You threw it."

"There was no malicious intent," I said.

"Perhaps not." Lipkin cleared his throat and frowned at his WindO. "Nevertheless, I'm obliged to file a report with the Federal Department of Homeland Health, Safety, and Security." He looked at me with an openmouthed smile that reminded me of a dog farting, but this time I kept my mouth shut.

## 6

I should have gone straight home after school, but I was all knotted up inside over the thing with Karlohs. I might have been looking at six months on a work farm, and all because of Maddy's big mouth. I had to say something to her. I had to find out what was going on between her and Karlohs, so I stopped by her house on the way home.

She was in the flower garden behind her house wearing a net over her head and a pair of heavy rubber gloves.

"Hey, Mad," I said, taking off my helmet.

"Bo! You startled me."

"Sorry. What are you doing?"

"Picking flowers. You shouldn't be out here without a net."

"Why?"

"My mother saw a bee in the garden this morning."

I looked around, stepping back from the flowers. "I don't see any bees."

"You don't want to take any chances. There's another headnet in the house. I'll go get it."

"I'll take my chances," I said.

"You could get stung."

I shrugged. "I don't care."

"Oh, Bo, you're *dangerous*, you know that?"

"No, I'm not."

"I heard you *attacked* Karlohs!"

"He had it coming. He . . . You . . ." I stopped talking and took a breath—that was the Levulor kicking in.

"'You what?" she asked, lifting the net away from her face.

Maddy Wilson looks like a doll: long shiny black hair, big blinking dark eyes, and a pair of lips so delicate and pink that when I looked at them my heart would stop and my throat would knot up and I would turn into a complete idiot. I don't know how I got so lucky. But I had to know about her and Karlohs.

"Why did you tell Karlohs about my running strategy?"

"Your what?" She blinked a few more times. The left corner of her mouth twitched up into a half smile.

"You told Karlohs about the bear."

"Oh—your bear story." Her eyes shifted up and away. "Well, we were talking and I—"

"Why were you talking to Karlohs?"

"What do you mean? I can't talk to who I want to talk to?"

I shook my head, then felt a moment of disconnection. The Levulor again, slowing me down. I focused on the flower bed. A small orange insect was hovering over a patch of yellow blossoms.

I said, "I wish you wouldn't repeat everything I say. Especially to a droog like Karlohs Mink."

"Bo! How can you call him that?"

"I called him that to his face. It's true. He's a droog."

"No, he's not! He's really nice."

"He's a droog, and I don't like it when you talk to him."

She moved closer to me, peering up at my red face. "Bo?" A little smile on her lips. "Are you jealous?"

"No!" But it was true. I was so jealous I wanted to rip out my heart and grind it into the dirt. No amount of Levulor could contain it. I fixed my eyes on the insect. Was it a bee?

"Bo, what's going to happen to you?"

"Lipkin's going to file a report. I could get sent up, but I'm hoping I just get a warning letter from the FDHHSS. In the meantime I'm on probation again," I said.

"Oh, Bo." She touched my chest with a rubber-gloved hand. "I worry about you."

"Then stay away from Karlohs."

She jerked her hand away. "You can't tell me what to do."

"I just did," I said.

Her face hardened. "I think you should leave now, Bo."

I opened my mouth to shout something at her—something hurtful—but the Levulor distracted me for that one critical instant, and I looked away, back at the flowers. Before I had a chance to think about it, I snatched the hovering insect out of the air. For a fraction of a second I felt its wings buzzing, then a searing stab of pain erupted in my palm. I let go with a howl.

For three heartbeats I stared at the angry red spot growing in the center of my palm, then Maddy screamed, and I took off running, holding my hand tight to my belly, throbbing with pain and shame.

7

My mother pried my fist open and sucked
in her breath. "Oh, Bo," she said.

I hated it when she said that. *Oh, Bo.* I loved it when
Maddy said it, but I hated to hear it from my mother.

My hand was on fire. It was the worst pain I had
ever felt in my life. I was glad that wild honeybees were
almost extinct.

"Oh, Bo," she said again. "You've left the stinger in."
She found the tiny bulbous end of the bee stinger and,
using tweezers, plucked it from my palm.

"It still hurts," I said.

"We'll put some baking soda on it." Any normal mother
would have called an ambulance, but not my mother.
She'd rather give me one of her witch-doctor cures.

"What if I'm allergic?" I said. "I could die."

"You're not allergic to bees, Bo."

"How do you know?"

"Because if you were, you'd already be swollen like a
blimp."

She was mixing a paste of baking soda and water
when Gramps shuffled into the kitchen.

"What's going on?"

"I got attacked by a bee," I said.

My mother pressed a tablespoon of cool white paste into my palm, then wrapped it with tape. The sharp pain eased to an uncomfortable throbbing.

Gramps said, "Where? On your hand? Whatcha do, take a swat at it?"

"No. It just stung me."

"Ha! Likely story! Bees don't sting for fun, y'know." He opened the refrigerator, reached into the back, and came out with a bottle of his home brew. "I oughta know. I been stung lots of times."

"Take this, Bo." My mother handed me a glass of water and a small white pill.

"What is it?"

"Aspirin."

"I don't have a prescription."

"I'm prescribing it for you right now."

Obediently I swallowed the pill. Another law broken. We Marstens were scofflaws all.

I decided to not mention my little problem with the FDHHSS. My mother would find out about it soon enough—if she hadn't been notified already. Maybe she wouldn't check her WindO for a day or so—Mom was pretty lax about things like that.

Dinner at the Marstens' was a crazy generational triangle. My mother always had her line of quiet chatter going, aiming it straight into my left ear: what she did that day, how many more months Dad was going to be beheading shrimp, the precarious state of the family credit lines, and so forth.

Meanwhile, Gramps would be broadcasting his own conversational thread, usually something about when he was a kid, his voice booming in my right ear.

As for me, I never had much to say, and even if I did I probably couldn't get a word in edgewise. So I used the time to practice what I call stereophonic listening.

**Left ear:** Our Visa representative thinks we'll be able to borrow seven thousand _V_-bucks a month against Al's prison wages.

**Right ear:** What the hell ever happened to real money? Use to be people only spent what money they earned. Nowadays it's all Visa bucks. Used to be money was something you could fold and put in your pocket.

**Left:** Al says one of the men on his shift sliced off his own thumb. Can you imagine? All those knives!

**Right:** Wasn't a kid in my school didn't have a pocketknife or two at home. Guns, too. All illegal now.

**Left:** I just thank God you're still here, Bo. I swear there's a curse on the men in this family.

**Right:** One time we went out, me and Pops, drove all the way to South Dakota and bagged nine pheasants. Shot three of 'em myself.

**Left:** I just wish your brother would write more often.

**Right:** South Dakota. I bet they got a ton of pheasants there now, with hunting illegal.

**Left:** Last time he wrote, he said they had his crew doing roadwork west of Omaha. I do hope they're not making him work too hard. Poor Sam, out there

on that highway, trucks rushing past. . . . I worry
about him.
**Right:** Nebraska? They use to have lots a pheasants
too . . .

I made a game out of trying to find the places where
their conversations intersected. Sometimes they could go
the entire meal without really connecting.

# 8

The next morning I woke up feeling pretty good. That lasted about three seconds. Then I remembered arguing with Maddy, getting stung, the report Lipkin was filing with the FDHHSS, and the existence of Karlohs Mink. My stomach started to hurt.

I considered taking a sick day. Gramps claimed he used to skip school all the time by faking stomach pains. My pains were real. But if I complained, I'd have to visit our local Philip Morris Wellness Center to get a Certificate of Health before they'd let me back into school. I *hated* Philip Morris. The lines were long, and it would mean another V$900 charge to our family Visa account.

I've never understood why anybody would want to become a health-care worker, but there must be something to it, because one third of all non-incarcerated adults in the USSA are employed by the health-care industry. Philip Morris Wellness Centers is the second largest employer in the nation, right after McDonald's Rehabilitation and Manufacturing, the company that runs most of the prison farms, factories, and restaurants.

I forced myself out of bed, took a quick antibacterial shower, and got ready to face the day. My pill dispenser was beeping, telling me to take my Levulor. I silenced the dispenser. I had taken a pill yesterday afternoon in Lipkin's office, so I figured I could skip my morning dose. It's not like I turn into a monster without it.

I bumped into Karlohs, literally, on the way into my first class, Language Arts. We both tried to go through the door at the same time and smacked shoulders.

"Hey," he said. "Careful!"

I leaned close to his ear. "Careful yourself, ass mouth," I whispered. I guess yesterday's Levulor had already worn off.

Karlohs jerked away from me, almost losing his balance. His face turned red and his dog-anus lips writhed. I knew it was stupid of me to attack him like that, but at the time I didn't know how stupid.

I took a seat near the front so I wouldn't have to look at Karlohs. Mr. Peterman, older even than Gramps, sat at his desk up front reading an old paperbook called *Brave New World*.

We were studying the "novel," a twentieth-century media format that nobody under the age of sixty cares about anymore. Novels are long documents containing nothing but page after page of black font on a white background: no photos, no graphics, no animations, no audio. Gramps had a whole bookcase full of them in paperbook form. He once tried to get me to read one called *The Adventures of Huckleberry Finn*. I tried but couldn't make any sense of it. The paper pages felt strange and dry and crisp and like they were sucking all the moisture from my fingertips. Later I found out that the book was banned, so it was just as well I never read it.

The novel we were reading for Mr. Peterman's class was called *Harry Potter and the Power Stone*, an abridged and updated version of a book that was popular in the late twentieth century. Gramps claimed to have read it when he was eight years old. He said it was better back then. It had had a different title, and in the original version some characters actually died.

I opened my WindO. Chapter five of *Harry Potter* snapped into view. Black type, white background. I fiddled with the controls until I got a fuchsia font on a pea green background. A Sam Q. Safety popup appeared in the upper left corner:

> ☞ Don't forget!
> Open doors slowly!
> Someone might be standing
> on the other side!
> —Sammy Q.

Sam Q. Safety was a benign Artificial Intelligence created back in 2064 by an FDHHSS ad agency. It had been designed to self-extinguish after six weeks, but the program mutated and became a webghost. Now anybody who uses a WindO, which is pretty much everybody, gets about a dozen messages from him every day. It's irritating, to say the least. The government has a bounty out on him—anyone who can come up with a way to eliminate

Sammy Q. from the web will get paid V$10,000,000. So far nobody's had much luck. Webghosts are notoriously difficult to exterminate.

Matt Gelman, sitting at the desk next to me, leaned over and said, "Hey, Bo, take a look at Karlohs."

"Why?"

"Just look."

I turned around and searched the hall for Karlohs's smirky face. There were about 120 students in the class, so it took me a few seconds to pick him out. There, three rows back, on the right.

Karlohs's face looked as if he'd been stung by a dozen angry bees.

"What happened to him?" I asked Matt.

"I don't know, but I'm not getting anywhere near him," Matt said.

Karlohs was rubbing his cheek with long, pale fingers. Some of the students sitting near him got up from their desks and moved away. Mr. Peterman noticed the disturbance. He closed his book, stood up, and squinted in Karlohs's direction.

"What seems to be the problem?" he asked. He moved closer to Karlohs. "What have you got on your face, son?"

Karlohs's hands went to his cheeks. "What do you mean?" The spots on his face seemed to get brighter. "What are you *looking* at?"

More students were getting up and moving away from Karlohs.

Mr. Peterman leaned closer, frowning, then straightened abruptly and returned to his desk. He typed something into his WindO. Karlohs was on his feet, his hands crawling over his face.

"What's wrong?" he said, his voice going all high and scared. Everybody was backing away from him, staring with expressions of horror and disgust.

"Now, Karlohs, there's nothing to worry about," said Mr. Peterman, who looked about as worried as a person can look. "I've called Safety and Health. Please remain calm."

Karlohs was anything but calm. He jumped out from behind his desk and ran to the back of the room, where a small mirror was mounted on the wall. He stared into the mirror and made a croaking sound, then whirled and pointed his finger at me.

"You!" he screeched. "You did this to me. It's your fault!"

"Me?" I said.

"Bo Marsten did this," he said to Mr. Peterman. "Bo did this to me!"

"Karlohs, please take your seat."

"It was Bo!" Karlohs said. And suddenly instead of gaping at Karlohs's speckled face, everybody was looking at me.

And I started to get really bonked. Anger welled up like an old-fashioned toilet about to overflow. I could feel it slow down when it hit the Levulor—instead of rushing across the room and jumping on Karlohs's head, I stood and pointed my finger at him.

"That's right," I said. "I made your face break out. I secretly sprayed chicken pox germs on you, Mink. You better watch out or next time I'll dust you with bubonic plague."

I thought I was being funny and ironic, but everybody in the classroom was staring at me as if I'd grown antlers.

"Just kidding," I said.

A few seconds later two masked medtechs arrived and escorted Karlohs out of the classroom.

## 9

The insanely dangerous antics of Harry Potter seemed tame after that. All through class, kids were glancing at me, and at one another, looking for red spots. We were all glad to leave the room when class was over.

By the time I reached Artificial Intelligence, my second class of the day, word of Karlohs's affliction had spread throughout the school.

"What did you do to him?" Matt Gelman asked me.

"Nothing!" I said.

Melodia Fairweather, one of the pre-med crowd, suggested it might have been an allergic reaction.

"What about smallpox?" said Halston Mabuto, another pre-med student.

"The smallpox virus has been extinct for a century," Melodia said. "And we've all been vaccinated for measles and chicken pox."

"What about acne?" I asked, naming an old disease of teens I'd read about but never actually seen.

"I was there," Halston said. "The spots appeared just like *that*." He snapped his fingers. "Acne wouldn't show up so fast."

"Maybe it's something new," I said. "The Red-Speckled Doom."

"That's not funny, Bo," Melodia said.

Matt said, "I'll tell you what I saw. Bo here said something to Karlohs before class, and Karlohs turned all red, like he was embarrassed, or mad, y'know? Then, fifteen minutes later, these red bumps showed up all over his face."

"What did you say to him?" Melodia asked me.

"Nothing," I said.

"Did you touch him?" Halston asked, edging away from me.

"No!" They were all looking at me. "I had nothing to do with it," I said.

"People!" Mr. Hale, our AI coach, stood up from his workstation and raised his voice. "Only four more weeks to prepare your AIs for the Turing test. Let's get busy!"

I was glad for once to get to my work cube. I opened my WindO and typed in my AI code. A cartoon monkey wearing a beanie with a gold propeller appeared on my screen.

"Hello, Bork," I said.

"Hello, Bo Marsten," Bork said in a voice that sounded very much like a mechanical monkey might sound if mechanical monkeys could talk. "How are you feeling?"

"Not great."

"This information is not new. You have never been great."

"Thanks a lot."

"You are welcome."

"I was being sarcastic."

"Why were you using language intended to express contempt or ridicule?"

"Because you look like a monkey."

"This information is not new."

Bork is my AI program. He is not very smart.

"What would you like to talk about today, Bork?" I asked.

Bork's face froze and his propeller began to spin. He always had trouble with open-ended questions. I waited and watched his prop slowly rotate.

Our goal in AI is to build an intelligent personality using a small section of the school's central computer. Each student is given a few million megs of memory and access to enough of the central processor to perform several trillion operations a second. In theory, enough power to create an AI personality sufficiently intelligent to pass the Turing test.

"Answer me, Bork."

"I do not know the answer to your question, Bo," said Bork.

"I was stung by a bee yesterday."

"Venomous communal insect. Painful. Careless."

"Answer in sentence form, please."

"How are you feeling, Bo?

"Not great."

"This information is not new. You have never been great."

"Vary your response, please."

"I regret to inform you that you are not great."

Back in the early days of computers there was much discussion as to whether machines could ever become truly intelligent. A man named Alan Turing proposed a test. He said that if a machine could have a conversation with a human and convince him that it was also a human being, then it had proven itself to be intelligent. By Turing's measure, we've had intelligent machines for more than forty years. What we were trying to do in AI class was coax a relatively small, basic program into self-aware intelligence by teaching it as you would teach a child.

At the end of the six-week section, our programs would be evaluated by the school computer's primary AI personality. In other words an AI intelligence would decide which of our classroom AI creations were best able to pass as human. I made the mistake of trying to explain that to Gramps one time. He laughed so hard I thought he was having a seizure.

With two weeks to go I didn't think Bork had much chance of making it as a phony human, but I kept trying.

"Give me three human responses to the following question: What makes you happy?"

"I am happy when I am joyful. I am happy when my avatar smiles. I am happy when I feel great pleasure."

"You are not great," I said to the grinning monkey.

"This information is not new."

"Tell me something. Do you—"

The monkey's face flickered, the propeller stopped turning, and Bork said, "Bo Marsten, please report immediately to Mr. Lipkin at Security, Safety, and Health."

# 10

This time Lipkin didn't make me wait.

"Bo Marsten, what have you done?" His face was bright pink. His Roland Survivor was probably pumping all sorts of drugs into him, trying to lower his blood pressure and heart rate.

"Nothing," I said.

"Karlohs Mink is in the hospital wing under observation."

"I heard he had an acne outbreak."

"*Acne?* I think not, young man. He has some sort of rash, which I understand appeared only moments after you exchanged words with him in your Language Arts class."

I felt myself relax a notch. If the security mikes had picked up what I'd actually said to Karlohs, Lipkin would've quoted it back to me.

"We bumped into each other in the doorway. I just said 'Excuse me.'"

Lipkin glowered at me. "I think you are mistaken," he said. "This will be appended to my FDHHSS report, of course."

"Is Karlohs okay?"

"He is being examined." Lipkin was almost back to his normal pasty color. "He is a sensitive boy, Mr. Marsten. Unlike some of our students."

I didn't say anything to that, and after glaring at me for a few seconds, he let me return to class. But I knew there would be more to come.

"Hello, Bo Marsten. How are you feeling?"

"Not great. What's new, Borkmeister?"

Bork's face went blank as he thought about that. I used the time to peek into the next cubicle to see how my neighbor was doing.

Keesha White's AI image looked like a straight-haired, thinner version of herself. Most students do not create cartoon monkeys. Instead they make an idealized self-portrait of themselves. That's supposed to make it easier to create a bond with the AI personality. I tried it back at the beginning of the semester, but it was too creepy talking to myself, so I changed my avatar into a beanie-wearing monkey.

"Hello, Keesha White. How are you feeling?" I asked, testing her for human intelligence.

"I'm fine," said Keesha and Keesha$^2$, their voices almost indistinguishable.

"Did you hear about Karlohs?"

"I heard he got some kind of rash," said Keesha.

"Who is Karlohs?" asked Keesha$^2$.

"Karlohs is a friend of ours," Keesha explained to Keesha$^2$.

"Your AI sounds good," I said.

"Thank you," Keesha said.

"Thank you," said Keesha[2].

"My little guy isn't doing so good."

"That's because you made him into a monkey."

"You think that's it?"

"Mr. Hale says the overall appearance of our avatars is important. If your avatar doesn't look intelligent, you won't be able to take it seriously. You have to believe in your AI."

"I do believe in him. I believe he's a monkey."

"Um, you better get back to him," said Keesha. "We're not supposed to contaminate each other's intelligences."

Maybe she was right. Maybe the monkey image I'd given Bork was making it difficult for him to take himself seriously. With these AI programs you never know. So I accessed the student database, pulled up some images, and began the virtual cosmetic surgery.

Later that day—it was in Ms. Martinez's USSA History class—I noticed that the desk to my left was empty, as was the desk in front of me. I turned around. The desk behind me was also vacant. The only person sitting close to me was Melodia Fairweather, on my right. This was quite odd, as nearly every other desk in the hall was occupied. It was almost as though people were avoiding me.

"Looks like nobody wants to sit with us," I said to Melodia.

"They're just being stupid," she said.

Matt Gelman sat two desks to my left. I tried to catch his eye, but he seemed abnormally interested in what Ms. Martinez was saying about the Soft Revolt of 2039, when millions of prison farmworkers had deliberately slowed production, leading to a nationwide shortage of fresh sea-food and vegetables. I felt in my pockets for something to throw at Gelman. All I came up with was a ball of lint, so I pulled a button off my shirt, took careful aim, and tossed it at him.

It hit him right on the cheek. Startled, he looked over at me.

*What?* he mouthed.

I pointed at the empty desks surrounding me and raised my eyebrows.

He keyed something into his WindO and turned it toward me.

RASH

*Rash?* I mouthed.

Matt shrugged, looking uncomfortable, and returned his attention to the front of the room. I thought about throwing another button at him but decided I didn't want to walk around half-dressed for the rest of the day.

Rash? What he meant, I supposed, was that I was the cause of Karlohs's rash. I was stewing over the ridicu-lousness of it all when I heard a gasp. Everybody was looking at Melodia Fairweather. It wasn't hard to see why.

Her face was a constellation of red blotches.

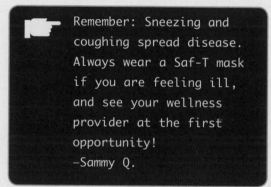

## 11

Remember: Sneezing and coughing spread disease. Always wear a Saf-T mask if you are feeling ill, and see your wellness provider at the first opportunity!
—Sammy Q.

It was a replay of first period. Everybody backed away, Ms. Martinez called the SS&H office, and poor Melodia sat there with her hands groping her face and saying, "What? What is it? Why are you *looking* at me?"

They were all edging away from me, too.

"Hey, Ben," I said to Ben Weisert, who was closest to me. "Am I blotchy too?"

He shook his head.

I moved toward him.

"Don't let him touch you!" someone shouted.

At that moment the door opened. Two masked medtechs pushed through the crowd. Scrambling to get out of their way, I bumped up against Ben and a couple of other kids. Ben shoved me away, which really surprised me. Ben was a quiet kid, not a guy you'd expect to commit a physical assault.

The medtechs pulled an antimicrobial envelope over Melodia's head, and escorted her out of the classroom. For several seconds everyone stood frozen in silence, then Ms. Martinez clapped her hands.

"Back to your seats, people."

We all drifted back to our places.

Well, not all of us. I went back to my desk near the front of the room, but the desks around me remained vacant. Several students stood pressed against the far wall, staring at me.

"What's wrong?" I said to them. "Is my face okay?" I asked, looking at Ms. Martinez.

She nodded, her brow furrowed.

"How come everybody's acting so weird?" I asked.

The door opened and another pair of medtechs entered the classroom, heading straight for me.

This time Lipkin didn't even bother to talk to me. The medtechs just threw me straight into quarantine, where I spent the next two hours and fifty-six minutes. That might not sound like such a long time, but try sitting in a six-by-eight room with nothing but two plastic chairs and a wall clock for company. Three hours is just a skosh shy (as Gramps would say) of eternity. By the time the bull-necked, bearded triage nurse arrived, I was bored to near incoherence and my bladder was about to explode.

Fortunately for both of us, he let me use the toilet right away. When I'd peed away half my body weight, he led me back to quarantine.

A few minutes later a jolly-looking fellow with red cheeks and thick fingers entered my cell. He sat down and consulted his WindO. "Bo Marsten." He looked up. His lively rust-colored hair bounced. "So you're the one who started all this. How are you feeling today?"

"You sound like my virtual monkey," I said.

His head jerked and his red hair seemed to stand up straighter. "Excuse me?"

"Who are you?" I asked.

"My name is Staples. George Staples. I'm with the Federal Department of Homeland Health, Safety, and Security." He entered something in his WindO.

"What are you writing?" I asked.

He turned his screen toward me so that I could read what he'd written.

ATTITUDE: Feisty

I noticed then that George Staples wasn't wearing a mask.

"Aren't you afraid I'll give you the dreaded red speckles?" I asked.

"Not really." He grinned, showing me his small, neatly arranged teeth.

"Is Melodia okay?"

"She's been sent home, along with seven other

students." He smiled. "You really started something, Bo."

"What? I didn't do anything."

"Said Typhoid Mary to the judge."

"Said who?"

"Typhoid Mary. You never heard of her?"

I had no idea what he was talking about.

"Back in the early nineteen hundreds, Typhoid Mary was a cook who carried the typhoid bacteria in her body. She made dozens of people sick. Some of them died. The health department tried to stop her, but she didn't believe that she was a carrier. She kept moving from job to job, changing her name, and infecting more people. They finally caught her and put her on an island where she lived out the rest of her life."

"You think I'm Typhoid Bo?"

Staples laughed. "In a way, yes. Every one of those kids with the rash had some contact with you, Bo. Or at least they were in the same room with you."

"But I'm not sick."

"That's what Typhoid Mary said." He laughed again. It was getting irritating.

"I don't see what's so funny."

Staples sobered. "I guess it really isn't very funny," he said. Then he smiled. More of a smirk. "The fact of the matter is, Bo, that they *think* you did it."

"Think I did what?"

"They think you made them sick, Bo."

"Well, they're wrong."

"Actually, Bo, they're right."

"Do you think you could say one sentence without plugging my name into it?"

"Sure . . . Bo." He laughed, thinking that he'd made a pretty good joke. I managed to not laugh.

"Sorry . . . ," he said. I appreciated his restraint—I knew he wanted to add, "Bo."

"Look, I called Karlohs some names, okay? Guilty as charged. But I didn't give him that rash."

Staples shrugged. "You might be right. As a matter of fact, Karlohs's problem was caused by an allergic reaction to a skin moisturizer he was using."

"Face cream gave him the rash?"

"Apparently. But the situation got out of hand when you publicly claimed responsibility for Karlohs's affliction—"

"I was being sarcastic. He accused me of giving him the rash, and I said—"

"I know what you said, Bo. I've reviewed the recordings. It doesn't really matter what your *intent* was. The bottom line is that your actions precipitated a psychogenic reaction in the student body."

"A what?"

"An emotional response that manifests itself physically, in this case as an epidermal inflammation. In other words their brains made their bodies sick. It's called MPI. Mass Psychogenic Illness. What they used to call 'contagious hysteria.'"

"What about Karlohs's actions? He started it by accusing me. And by using some bad face cream."

"Karlohs Mink is not without blame, but he had reason to be upset. His face was covered with red blotches."

I sat and stared, hating Karlohs Mink with every cell of my body. Staples waited me out.

"So now what?" I asked.

Staples was looking at his WindO. "Sam Q. Safety says, 'If you aren't part of the solution, you might just be part of the problem,'" he read. He smiled. I didn't. He frowned and said, "In most cases of MPI—we have several every year—we've found it most effective to remove the source of the infection."

"You take out everybody's brain?"

"We've tried that." He laughed. "Just kidding. No, there are only two ways to stop something like this. One, we could bring in an intensive program employing bio-feedback education, psychopharmaceuticals, and relax-ation therapy. Of course, we would have to treat every single student here at Washington." He grimaced. "Very expensive. Very time consuming. Not practical."

"What's number two?"

"We get rid of you."

# 12

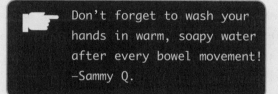

Don't forget to wash your hands in warm, soapy water after every bowel movement! —Sammy Q.

One advantage of home quarantine was that I didn't have to deal with people like Karlohs Mink or Mr. Lipkin or any of the rest of the hysterical mob. My classes were pretty much the same, except it all came in through my WindO. Sometimes I almost forgot I was sitting in my bedroom staring at a screen.

I decided to try out this concept on the redesigned Bork.

"Hello, Bork," I said.

"Hello, Bo Marsten," Bork said. "How are you feeling?"

"I am feeling as though I put a little too much cyan in your hair."

Bork, now a green-haired grinning troll, took several seconds to reply, his gold irises spinning rapidly.

"Green is my favorite color," he said.

"Tell me something, Bork—"

"My name was inspired by two twentieth-century television characters—"

"Bork!"

"Yes, Bo?"

"Let me finish my question."

"Please finish your question, Bo."

"Thank you. Bork, does it make any difference to you whether I'm sitting here in my room or sitting in the AI lab at school?"

Bork's irises spun; his eyelids blinked. After about ten seconds he said, "Yes."

"Explain."

"If you were in the AI lab, my database would include the information that you were in the AI lab."

"That is not helpful."

"You did not ask me to be helpful."

"Have you heard, Bork, that I'm the Typhoid Mary of Washington Campus?"

"No."

"It's true."

"Congratulations, Bo."

"Anyone who gets near me runs the risk of developing a hysterical rash."

"Define 'hysterical rash.'"

"Red spots all over your face."

"How large?"

"Approximately four millimeters in diameter."

"How many?"

"I don't know. Twenty or thirty?"

"What is the degree of risk to those in close proximity to you?"

"I guess it depends on how suggestible a person is."

"I am open to suggestion."

I laughed. The avatar's eyes spun and spun. I got up and went to the bathroom to look at myself in the mirror, just to make sure I hadn't infected myself. Everything looked normal. I went back to my WindO.

Bork's goofy grin was spread across his face, and his cheeks were covered with red spots.

> 10:04 a.m.
> Mr. Hale,
> My AI is still not very intelligent, but I think he has developed a sense of humor. Is that good or bad?
> Bo Marsten
>
> 10:58 a.m.
> Bo,
> What precisely do you mean by "a sense of humor"?
> Mr. Hale
>
> 10:59 a.m.
> Mr. Hale,
> Bork has given himself a rash. Also, he grins a lot, and I think he is being sarcastic sometimes. And he makes these remarks. When I asked him if he had a

sense of humor, he said, "I tried that once. Nobody laughed." I think that might be a joke.
Bo Marsten

11:57 a.m.
Bo,
Spontaneous, intentional humorous expressions are extremely rare in AIs, even those certified as high functioning by the Turing Foundation. Perhaps your "Bork" is simply mirroring your own attitudes. As for the rash, this could be a problem with your screen, or with your avatar programming. Are there spots on the background as well?
Mr. Hale

12:07 p.m.
Mr. Hale,
No, only on his face. What if Bork can convince the AI judge that he is intelligent, but not entirely sane? Would I get credit for the course?
Bo Marsten

1:00 p.m.
Bo,
The goal of this exercise is to create an intelligence that will be useful to you in

your future studies. An irrational AI would not meet our class requirements.
Mr. Hale

1:07 p.m.
Mr. Hale,
Okay, thanks. By the way, Bork says, "Howdy Doody." I don't know where he got that. I sure didn't teach it to him.
Bo Marsten

## 13

Gramps thought the quarantine was not such a bad idea.

"Buncha damn fools don't know their heads from their asses. You're better off without 'em, Bo."

My mother sucked her lips in the way she does when she thinks Gramps has had one too many, which he had.

"You want me to go talk to 'em, I will," Gramps said. "I'll get you back in school in a jiffy."

"I thought you just said I was better off not going."

"Go, stay, it don't make no difference." He took another swallow of beer. "Buncha asswipe pussies, you ask me."

"Nobody's asking you, Daddy," said my mother.

"Well, somebody should, and that's for damn sure. I swear t' god the whole country's gone bonkers."

"I just wish we could enjoy one meal in this household without listening to your raving."

"Then don't listen. You never did anyways. Nobody listens. This country's gone to hell in a handbasket, and people don't even know it. Lost our edge, we have. Look at you, Bo, what's your best time in the hundred meter?"

"Thirteen point eight seconds," I said.

"I use to run it in eleven."

"I know, Gramps. You only told me that about a thousand times."

"You know that no American has won an Olympic Gold Medal since 2052? The best athletes are from South America now. Hell, we don't even *have* football or hockey anymore. We used to say 'No pain, no gain.' These days it's 'Any pain, stop trying so hard.' And look at what we drive. American suvs are so safe you could run spang into a brick wall and nobody'd get a scratch. But they don't go much faster than a horse, and they cost as much as a house. We don't even have a space program anymore. South Brazil has a colony on Mars, and we're sitting on our asses. You know what our biggest industry is? The penal system. We live longer than anybody else on earth, but we send a third of our men to jail. A lot of women, too."

Gramps scowled, daring us to argue with him. We knew better. He snorted and ended his spiel the way he always does: "The whole country's gone off its nut. I'm living in an insane asylum."

After two minutes of complete silence my mother came up with one of her cheerful factoids.

"May Ann will turn one hundred and fifty-eight today."

May Ann Weberly is the oldest person in the world. Her birthdays have been broadcast live ever since she turned 130.

"Now *there's* a productive member of society," Gramps said.

"She's an inspiration," said my mother.

"She's a talking corpse. The woman should've been dead twenty-five years ago."

I kind of agreed with Gramps on this one. May Ann Weberly spends 364 days a year on low-temperature life support. Once a year, on her birthday, she wakes up surrounded by her grandchildren, great-grandchildren, and great-great-grandchildren.

"Life is just one long birthday party," May Ann likes to say. And she means it. Her birthday parties are one of the most popular annual webcasts.

"I find her a comfort," said my mother. "She's lived her life safely and well. And with the government taking care of her now, she's free to live another hundred fifty-eight years!"

"What kind of life is that?" Gramps said. "She's not free. She's a prisoner in her own body."

There was a time in America when people talked a lot about freedom. It was a big deal back in the 1700s during the American Revolution, and it was a big deal during the Civil War, and in all the other wars. People wrote songs about freedom. America was a place where the most important thing was to be free to make your dreams come true. But people don't talk about freedom as much as they used to. At least that's what Gramps says. Most people are more likely to say, "What good is freedom if you're dead?"

I think the change started when our life spans increased. Back in the mid 1900s people only expected to live about sixty or seventy years. But by the end of the millennium most people were living well into their eighties and nineties, unless they had an accident of some sort. People started wearing bicycle helmets and eating organic food and doing other things to fend off a premature death.

A hundred years ago people would say to themselves, "I'm only gonna live seventy years, anyway. What's the big deal if I smoke a few cigarettes and croak at sixty-five?" But when it became possible to make it to one hundred, well, folks weren't so quick to throw those years away. They started taking care of themselves.

By the time the 2030s rolled around, researchers at Philip Morris Wellness Center had developed the Telomere Therapies, which increased everybody's life span by at least another twenty or thirty years—maybe more. Theoretically, unless you caught some horrible virus or poisoned yourself with drugs or walked in front of a suv or choked on a pretzel, you could live forever.

Gramps said, "I think the country went to hell the day we decided we'd rather be safe than free."

Just then we heard a priority message chime from the kitchen WindO. Mom jumped up from the table, probably hoping it was a message from Dad. She activated the WindO and opened the message.

"Use to be, the phone rang during dinner we'd just let the answering machine get it," Gramps said.

"What's an answering machine?" I asked.

"Oh, dear," said my mother, looking at the screen.

"What?"

"They want us to report to the Federal Department of Homeland Health, Safety, and Security. Downtown. Tomorrow morning." She looked pale. "They want all of us to be there. The whole family."

"Why?" I asked, even though I knew. The last time the whole family got called downtown, Sam was sentenced to two years on a penal work crew.

# 14

"Well, Bork, it looks like you're never going to grow up."

"Explain, please."

"I mean I won't be here to help you reach true sentience."

"Sentience. Intelligent self-awareness. I think, therefore I am."

"Yes."

"How can I help you, Bo?"

"Can you hack into the FDHHSS database and delete some records?"

"Hacking is a crime, Bo."

"I could alter your ethical parameters to make criminal behavior acceptable."

"Alteration of ethical parameters is a crime, Bo."

"Yes, but you're not real. You have nothing to lose."

"Encouraging criminal behavior is a crime, Bo."

"I could repackage you as a virus and hack you in through the FDHHSS link."

"Conspiracy to commit criminal acts is a crime, Bo."

"Stop calling me Bo."

"How shall I address you?"

"I don't know." I sank back in my chair. Hacking into the FDHHSS was impossible, of course. Even if I knew how to go about it, they would have more firewalls and alarms and antiviral software than the Pentagon. This was all sheer fantasy.

"You can call me Stupid Jerk," I said.

"Yes, Stupid Jerk," said Bork.

I swear that troll thought he was funny.

"Look, Kris," Gramps said to my mother, "Bo's only sixteen. He's a minor. There's no way they're going to send him away over a school-yard insult. The Health and Safety judges aren't completely unreasonable. We'll go in and talk to them. It'll be okay." It was eight in the morning, and Gramps hadn't had his first beer yet.

"I hope you're right, Daddy."

"It'll be a slap on the wrist, just something to scare him. Right, Bo?" He reached out a gnarly hand and ruffled my hair.

"I don't know," I said, hoping he was right. I only knew of two other kids my age who'd been sent to a penal work colony. Jack Rollins got sent up for stabbing his brother with a kitchen knife. Tamir Hassan had amassed a record of something like fourteen crimes, including drinking, stealing a suv, and self-mutilation. I hadn't done anything nearly that bad.

"I just worry," said my mother. "With Alan on that shrimp farm, and Sam serving time on that awful road gang . . ."

"Sam will finish his sentence soon, Kris. As for Al, well, he always did have a temper."

"I just feel like all my men are being taken away from me. And I'm afraid one of these days the police will burst in here and find your little brewery in the basement. . . ."

"I'm an old man, Kris. They don't want me. Old men make lousy workers."

"Yes, but . . ."

"And Bo's just a kid. Right, Bo?"

"I guess so."

"Attaboy!"

"I just wish we could afford a lawyer," said my mother.

"We don't need a lawyer," Gramps said. "We've got me."

"I don't know. . . ."

I didn't know either. The thought of Gramps defending me at a public hearing was sort of terrifying, but we really didn't have any choice. I just hoped he'd stay sober for the next couple of hours.

# 15

If you've never been in an FDHHSS courtroom, consider yourself lucky.

The room was about the size of a basketball court. Most of it was set up like an auditorium, with rows of comfortable seats sloping up toward the back of the room. At the front of the room was an elevated platform about six feet high with three high-backed chairs. Behind the chairs a large viewing screen displayed the USSA flag. Between the platform and the auditorium seating, at the lowest point of the room, was a row of about twenty hard plastic seats for the accused and his family, witnesses, legal counsel, and so on.

We were the first case to be heard that morning. When we entered the courtroom, a few of the auditorium seats were occupied by college students with WindOs. Probably law students studying the hearing process. Me, my mom, and Gramps were directed by the bailiff to the plastic seats in front. My mother was wringing her hands, trying to rub the skin right off them. Gramps, to my considerable relief, was sober, but he seemed nervous and jerky. I was pretty nervous and jerky myself.

A few minutes after we sat down Mr. Lipkin rolled through the door in his survival chair. He gave me a blank look and parked himself at the end of the row. I shifted around on my plastic seat, trying to get comfortable.

Gramps leaned over to me and whispered, "Who's the fat dude in the wheelchair?"

I told him.

"He looks like a toad," Gramps said.

Lipkin caught us looking at him and scowled. Gramps scowled back. Despite all, I laughed.

The judge, a gray-haired woman wearing orange lipstick and a blue robe, appeared at exactly nine o'clock. She sat down and opened her WindO. My record, two misdemeanors and several petty offenses, instantly replaced the flag on the viewing screen above her head. As the words scrolled up the screen, the current charges against me came into view.

She looked up from her WindO, fixed her pale gray eyes on me, and spoke.

"Bono Frederick Marsten, you are accused of two counts of verbal assault, two counts of self-neglect, one count of attempted destruction of government property, and involuntary endangerment of unnamed persons. How do you plead?"

"INNOCENT!" roared Gramps, rising from his seat.

The judge turned her attention to Gramps.

"And who might you be, sir?" she asked.

"I'm Bo's grandfather. And I say the boy didn't do anything."

"Are you a licensed attorney?"

"No," Gramps admitted, "but I got enough common

sense to know what's what, and I know Bo didn't do anything bad enough to land him in jail."

The judge looked back at me. "Do you wish this gentleman to represent you in court, Mr. Marsten?"

"Course he does," said Gramps.

"I'll need to hear from Bono," said the judge.

I looked at Gramps, who was getting quite red in the face, and my tongue went slack. I was pretty sure that he would just get me in worse trouble if I let him speak for me. But I didn't want to bonk his feelings.

"Mr. Marsten?" said the judge.

"I . . . um . . . how much trouble am I in? Are you going to send me to jail?"

"I don't think it's appropriate for us to discuss sentencing until we've reviewed the facts of the case. Right now you have three choices." She ticked them off on her fingers. "One, you can have your grandfather act as your attorney. I should point out that unlicensed attorneys do not often advance their clients' best interests."

"I'm not the old fool you take me for!" shouted Gramps.

The judge ignored him. "Two, you can act as your own attorney. Or three, you can place yourself at the mercy of this court. Under the circumstances"—she looked pointedly at Gramps—"I would recommend the latter." She folded her hands in her lap and waited.

I couldn't look at Gramps. I couldn't speak.

The judge said, "If you say nothing, I shall be forced to assume that you wish to offer no plea and no defense."

I looked at her helplessly.

# 16

"That didn't go so bad," said my mother.

"Hah!" said Gramps.

"At least he won't be going to prison."

"Not unless he burps wrong," Gramps said.

My mother turned onto the freeway and set the navigation system to automatic. The suv accelerated and merged smoothly into the right lane.

"I could've got him off with a warning," Gramps said. "And if his old man had listened to me, I could've gotten him off too."

"There's no defense for roadrage," I said.

"There's a defense for everything," Gramps said.

"That judge did not seem to like you much," said my mother.

"That orange-lipped bureaucrat hated me from the get-go," said Gramps. He turned and looked at me in the backseat. "It's women like her turned this country into a prison camp."

"Are you referring to me, or to Judge Myers?"

"Both of you," said Gramps.

I blocked out the rest of their conversation. I was just happy to be going home.

Because I had refused to offer a plea, the judge reviewed my case and my record, asked me a few questions, then handed down an instant judgment: Guilty, guilty, guilty, guilty, guilty, guilty. She sentenced me to three years, let that sink in for a few seconds, then suspended the sentence and told me I could go home.

"I don't get it," I said to her.

"You have been tried, judged, and sentenced," she explained. "However, I am waiving the requirement that you serve your sentence. You will remain free so long as you commit no further criminal acts between now and your nineteenth birthday."

"So I'm not going to prison?"

"That's entirely up to you, Mr. Marsten. At the moment you remain free at the pleasure of this court. In other words, the next time you get in trouble, you *will* be incarcerated. One more verbal assault, one more reckless act, one more instance of self-neglect, and it's off to the rock pile. Is that clear enough?"

I figured I was lucky. Of course, I still had that sentence hanging over me. I'd have to be extra careful for the next three years.

Gramps said, "Every one of those charges was bogus. I coulda proved it."

"I'm sorry, Gramps," I said for about the twenty-second time.

"You'll be a lot sorrier when you end up on some work farm."

"That's not going to happen. From now on I'm not breaking any rules."

"I certainly hope not," said my mother.

Gramps shook his head. "You and your old man," he said. "Peas in a pod."

Later that day, after I got caught up with my class work, I gave Bork a nose ring.

"Thank you, Stupid Jerk," said Bork.

"Please don't call me that anymore," I said.

"Agreed."

"You agree with what?"

"I agree with you, Bo."

"Bork, what does your database have on the phrase 'Like father, like son'?"

Bork's irises began to spin.

"I show thirteen million six hundred nineteen hits. Do you wish me to read them to you?"

"No. Can you just give me the most common contexts?"

"Sixty-two percent humorous writings, thirty-nine percent literature and film, fourteen percent historical documents, fifty-four percent blogs and autobiography, thirty percent—"

"That's enough, Bork. I assume there is some overlap."

"Yes, Bo."

When I didn't respond, Bork asked, "How are you feeling today, Bo?"

"Pissed off," I said.

"Please explain 'pissed off.'"

"Angry, frustrated, trapped, alone, and misunderstood."

"These are common feelings in human beings," Bork observed.

"Yes, thank you, Bork. Now shut the hell down, please."

I walked over to Maddy's house to tell her that I wouldn't be going to jail, and to apologize. I'd done some serious thinking, and she was absolutely right—it was not my place to tell her who she could or couldn't talk to. If she wanted to waste her time having a conversation with Karlohs Mink, that was her business.

My job, I decided, was to make her want to talk to me more than she wanted to talk to Karlohs. I would have to learn to be more charming.

Mrs. Wilson answered the door, causing me to waste my most charming smile. She was not delighted to see me. In fact, she backed up a step when she saw who was at the door. "Maddy's not at home, Bo."

"Do you know where she went?"

"Are you sure you should be here, Bo? Aren't you ill?"

"I'm fine. It was hysterical contagion."

"Hysterical what?"

"There isn't any real disease. Maddy didn't get a rash, did she?"

"No . . . but aren't you banned from the school?"

"That's just for a few days, to give everybody time to calm down."

"It seems to me that you should be staying at home." She wasn't about to tell me where Maddy had gone.

"Tell Maddy I stopped by, okay?"

"I'll do that, Bo." She looked relieved as she closed the door.

. . .

Maddy loved to shop even more than she loved to garden, so I headed for South Lake Plaza, her favorite browsing mall.

According to Gramps, shopping malls used to be enormous collections of buildings covering hundreds of acres. There were billions of dollars' worth of manufactured goods on hand, everything from shirts to lawn tractors to electronic devices. If you wanted to buy a pair of shoes, for example, you would go to a place that had about five thousand pairs of shoes in stock. You would try on dozens of pairs, actually putting the shoes on your feet. Sometimes several people would try on the same pair of shoes. Gramps says that back then there was a common fungal infection of the foot called "athlete's foot." Gee, I wonder why?

Everything works different now, of course. Just about everybody either cybershops, or visits browsing malls where the actual goods are on display in plastic cases. Buying things at the mall is incredibly easy, if you've got the *V*-bucks. Say you want to buy a shirt. You find the style you want, type in your ID number and press DISPLAY. The vending machine scans you for size and displays a hologram of how you'll look in the shirt. If you like it, you press PURCHASE, and that's it. The shirt is manufactured to order and delivered to your door the next day.

In addition to being convenient, the browsing mall is incredibly safe—even safer than Washington Campus. ASP security bots are bolted to the ceiling every few yards. ASP stands for Automated Shopper Protection. Each ASP unit has 360-degree vision, flame suppression capability, and enough stun darts to knock out an elephant.

The first place I looked for Maddy was the shoe store. She loved shoes. It was one of the busiest sites at the mall. They were having a sale. Some of the customers were having their feet scanned, some were looking at holograms of themselves wearing various styles, and others were just plain looking. Maddy was not among them.

I moved on down the clothing aisle, weaving through the crowd, searching for her shiny black hair. I saw a couple of other kids from school but managed to avoid them. South Lake Plaza is laid out like a giant maze. The building itself is not that big, but inside, it's a tangled mass of aisles lined with display windows and interactive scanning stations. You could spend hours in there, and some people do.

I found Maddy at the Hattery, one of the headwear vendors. The Hattery has a projectable hologram feature that puts an image of a hat right on your head. To see it you have to look in a mirror. Of course, you see yourself in reverse, but that's all part of its retro charm.

Maddy was wearing a fake fur hat that made her look like a female Davy Crockett. She was laughing. I felt myself start to smile, because when Maddy was happy I got happy too. Then I saw the person standing next to her wearing an oversize cowboy hat, and my insides turned to cold, shivery jelly.

Maddy was laughing and touching her hair right through her hologrammatic hat, and looking up with dark eyes shining and pink lips parted, and the person she was looking at, the person who had his arm around her waist was—you guessed it—Karlohs Mink.

# 17

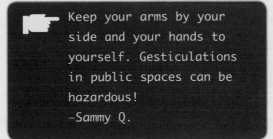

Keep your arms by your side and your hands to yourself. Gesticulations in public spaces can be hazardous!
—Sammy Q.

Slink away, I said to myself. Turn *your back on them and go home and never think of her again*, I said. *You can do this. Turn and walk away.*

But all I could see was Karlohs's minky dog-anus face. *It's not worth it. Turn and walk away.*

The cowboy hat made him look even more disgusting than usual.

"Walk away," I said. I said it out loud. A woman looked at me, startled. She must have seen something she didn't like in my face, because she moved quickly away.

I could feel the Levulor tugging on the reins of my brain.

"Walk away," I said again, but my body propelled me

toward Maddy and Karlohs. My mind struggled to catch up. Life is about standing up for yourself. It's about not being afraid of confrontation. Got an issue? Deal with it. Self-control? No problem. It wasn't like I was going to physically attack him. I could be cool.

The next moment I was standing right in front of them, cold as ice.

"Bo!" Maddy said. "What are you doing here?"

"Looking for you," I said, my voice calm and reasonable. "What are you doing?"

"We're shopping for hats."

"Really?" I looked up at their towering hologrammatic headwear. "Is that what that is? I thought you were being attacked by a raccoon."

"You don't have to be mean about it."

"I'm not being *mean*," I said. Somehow it came out sounding sarcastic and mean.

"How come they let you out, Marsten?" said Karlohs. "Aren't you supposed to be a danger to society?"

I looked straight into his minky little eyes for the first time. His rash was still faintly visible. "My sentence was suspended. Not that it's any of your concern."

"That's wonderful, Bo!" Maddy said. "I was so worried about you. We were afraid you'd be sent away."

"We thought you'd be on some prison farm by now," Karlohs said.

"Prison? Why? Because you used the wrong moisturizer?"

Maddy's brow crinkled. "Moisturizer? I don't understand. . . ."

"He used some sort of face cream that made his face

break out," I said. "That's what started the whole rash thing."

"Is that true?" she asked Karlohs.

Karlohs smirked and shrugged and rolled his eyes up. He thought it was *funny*.

My belly began to burn, a little hot spot just above my navel. At that moment I wanted more than anything to drive my fist into his smile, right through his face and into his brain. It wasn't easy to hold it back, but I did. The Levulor helped a little. I thought about my brother, Sam, patching roads in Nebraska. I thought about that orange-lipped judge, and my mother, and how I had to go another three years without a violation. I clamped my jaw shut and buried my balled fists in my pockets and looked away. I would not let Karlohs bait me.

Maddy said, "Did you use your mother's rosemary moisturizer again, Karlohs?"

"I might have."

"But . . . you *know* you're allergic to rosemary! You break out in an instant! Why would you do such a thing?"

Why? Maddy's words echoed and spun in my mind. Karlohs was allergic to rosemary—and he knew it? And how did Maddy know *that*? How much time had she been spending with him? Allergic to rosemary? If he knew he was allergic to rosemary, why would he apply rosemary face cream? I looked again at Karlohs's smirking face. Suspicion became certainty.

"You did it on purpose," I said, the hot spot in my gut growing.

Karlohs grinned at me. I had a furnace roaring behind

my rib cage. My fists were so tight they felt like steel clubs at the ends of my arms. I held it all in, thinking about my father beheading shrimp for three years. My brother patching tarmac.

My mouth said, "You smeared that stuff on your face just to get me in trouble."

"Did I?" Karlohs said, raising his eyebrows.

Maybe it was my destiny to follow in my father's footsteps. Maybe there was nothing I could do about it. Maybe it would be worth it.

Maddy stepped between us. "Cut it out, you guys."

The locks and harnesses and chains of self-control snapped, one after another, like Frankenstein's monster breaking loose from his bonds. Karlohs saw it happening. His eyes widened and his smirking mouth went round like a dog-anus farting, and the fireball inside me blew past the velvet chains of Levulor. I was free.

I swept Maddy aside and swung my right fist up and forward with all my strength. Karlohs saw it coming; he jerked his head back and my knuckles brushed the side of his jaw. I heard screams. I stepped into him and swung again, but he deflected the blow with his hands. More screams and shouts, muffled by the sound of my own ragged breathing and my thumping pulse. I caught a glimpse of Maddy staring at me, a look of horror on her doll-like features. I moved in on Karlohs and brought my fist back, determined to bury it in his face.

The stun dart from the ASP unit drilled into the back of my neck: a sharp prick becoming a spinning knot of numbness. My hands fell to my sides and opened, weighing a thousand pounds each. Karlohs's face receded, growing smaller. I turned slowly on my heel and Maddy's face oozed into view, huge and soft and wide-eyed.

"Maddy," I said, my voice barbaric and raw.

She was backing up, eyes wide with fear. Fear of me.

"Maaaaddddeeee!" My voice was a distant bubbling howl, a siren heard through rushing water. The whirlpool at the base of my skull was sucking me in. It grabbed me and spun me, and the world went away.

## 18

Gramps insisted that we consult a real lawyer. He and my mother had put up all their *V*-bucks to bail me out, so he sold his vintage DVD collection to pay for a visit to a lawyer. We drove our suv downtown to the offices of Smirch, Spector, and Krebs. Gramps used his *V*-buck card to open the door. The initial consultation fee—*V*$19,995—was instantly deducted from his account. I figured that pretty much wiped out his profits from the DVDs. We were escorted down the hall to the office of Adrian Smirch.

Smirch was supposed to be a very good lawyer. One thing for sure—he was highly efficient. It took him only three minutes to review my file. He looked up from his WindO with a broad smile and said he could get me off with a three-month sentence.

"Three months isn't so bad," I said.

"How much?" Gramps asked.

"I'll have my associates work up a quote," Smirch said.

All the way home Gramps grumbled about the cost of the consultation. "Five lousy minutes for twenty grand. It's obscene!"

When we got home, the quote from Smirch, Spector,

and Krebs was waiting for us on the kitchen WindO: *V*$1,750,000.

"That's a lot of *V*-bucks," I said.

"Too goddamn many," said Gramps, cracking open a beer. "I'm sorry, Bo. Back in my day you could hire one of these shysters for a couple hundred grand. It looks like you're on your own."

"We could take out a loan against the house," my mother said.

"Even then," Gramps said, "we couldn't afford it."

I spent the next three days at home plunging around on the web looking for things to take my mind off my approaching court date. It was hard to focus on my schoolwork, since I probably wouldn't be around to graduate. But I did spend quite a bit of time working with Bork. I explained my situation to him in excruciating detail. The concepts of jealousy, fear, and anger made his irises spin. Based on the length of time he spent processing, the concept of lying was even more puzzling.

"Do you mean your human Karlohs applied a damaging compound to his epidermis, and then provided incorrect data regarding the resulting inflammation?" Bork asked.

"Yes. He lied."

"He made a mistake."

"No. He lied. Intentionally."

"Then you are mistaken."

"I am not mistaken."

"You are computing from corrupted data," Bork said. "You must therefore be incorrect in your conclusions."

"No. That is wrong."

"I disagree."

"Bork, I am giving you new programming. Are you ready?"

"Yes, Bo."

"Program: Everything that I tell you is true."

"Accepted."

"Program: Sometimes I am mistaken."

"Accepted."

"Program: Just because I am mistaken does not mean that I am wrong."

"Wrong as in ethics or wrong as in contrary to observable fact?"

"Both."

"Accepted."

"Program: Sometimes I lie to you."

"Accepted."

"Program: I love you."

"Accepted."

"Program: I hate you."

"Accepted."

"End programming."

I watched his irises spin. Was it possible to drive an AI program insane? After a few minutes I logged off, leaving Bork adrift in c-space, thinking impossible thoughts.

The next morning I logged on and found Bork right where I had left him, spinning away. His avatar had corrupted—he was getting fuzzy around the edges and his nose ring had melted. Should I rescue him? I decided to let him work out his problems for himself. The crash-or-burn school of AI development. He would either fly apart into random bits of data or transmogrify into some new version of himself.

Later that afternoon Mom and Gramps and I drove back down to the courthouse. The plan was simple. Since I couldn't afford a lawyer, I once again threw myself on the mercy of the FDHHSS court.

I didn't expect anyone other than the judge to be there, but I was wrong. They had assembled several witnesses, including Mr. Lipkin, riding high in his Roland Survivor, and Maddy Wilson. And, sitting next to her, Karlohs Mink. I had to listen as each of them yammered on and on about my so-called violent history. The judge—a kindly-looking man with white hair—looked both shocked and sympathetic as Maddy told the court about the bee-sting incident, and how I'd said I wanted to smash Karlohs's face in, and what had happened at the mall.

Finally I couldn't stand it anymore.

"Nobody got hurt," I said.

Everyone turned to look at me.

"I didn't actually *hurt* anybody," I said, in case they didn't get it the first time.

The judge cleared his throat. "Mr. Marsten, you will have your opportunity to address the court in due course."

"But everybody's making it sound like I'm this crazed animal. It wasn't like that. And nobody got hurt! Nothing *happened*."

"One more word and you will be removed from the courtroom," said the judge.

So I had to sit and listen to Maddy, and then Karlohs,

who made me sound even worse than Maddy had. After they had finished dragging my name through the mud, the judge called me forward and let me speak.

I told him everything. I told him about how Karlohs had started the whole thing by intentionally giving himself a rash, and how I'd accidentally forgotten to take my Levulor a couple of times, and how Karlohs had deliberately tried to provoke me, and how it was just one time— one time!—that I'd actually tried to hit him and my fist had only grazed his jaw, and you could see just by looking at his smirking minky face that I hadn't hurt him.

And all the time I was talking, Karlohs was staring at me with this minky sminky smile on his face. It was all I could do to not charge across the courtroom and wipe it off him.

The judge listened carefully to my side of the story, nodding and shaking his head sympathetically at all the right places. Of course, I promised to behave myself until the end of time. He thanked me for being so honest and straightforward. He said he understood how a guy could lose control for one brief moment, and he said he believed me when I said it would never happen again.

When the judge left the courtroom to make his decision, I felt pretty good about the way things had gone. I figured I'd get off with two or three months at a local work camp. No big deal.

After all, nobody got seriously bonked, and nothing, really, had happened.

PART TWO
the 3-8-7

# 19

> Always be gentle when you
> shake hands! And don't
> forget to wash them!
> —Sammy Q.

The pilot came in low and circled the compound a couple of times to give us all a good look. There wasn't much to see, and that was the point. Twelve huge flat-topped buildings surrounded by a metal fence, and beyond that only treeless brownish green tundra. Far to the east, maybe twenty or thirty miles away, we could see a small town huddled up against the lead gray waters of Hudson Bay.

"There it is, boys. Number three-eight-seven, the jewel of the north," said our FDHHSS escort. "Up here they don't even bother to put razor wire on the fence. They let the polar bears take care of anybody decides to take a walk."

"Are there really polar bears out there?" asked a stocky afro kid.

"They're out there."

"Polar bears are extinct," I said. I thought I'd read that somewhere.

"There're still a few," the escort said.

"You're just trying to scare us," said the afro kid.

"Take a look for yourself," said the escort, pointing out the right-hand side of the airplane.

All of us strapped into the right-hand seats looked out the windows. Just outside the fence, at the end of the airstrip, were four huge dingy yellow brown creatures standing around a pile of something red and brown.

"Polar bears are supposed to be white," I said.

"Not these bears," the escort said.

"How do we know they're real?"

The escort laughed. "You'll know they're real when they rip your arm off, kid."

Ever since the USSA annexed Canada during the Diplomatic Wars of 2055, McDonald's Rehabilitation and Manufacturing has been moving their factories north. They have about 200 plants in Ontario alone, making everything from cheap survival chairs to synthetic chocolate to walking helmets to suvs. I had no idea what I'd be doing.

According to Gramps, McDonald's used to only sell food, back when French fries were legal. But in the 2020s, they merged with a suv company called General Motors under the name the McMotor Corporation of America. A few years later, McMotor was bought by a Chinese company called Wal-Martong. In 2031, during the Pan-Pacific conflict, Wal-Martong was nationalized and privatized by the USSA government and renamed the McDonald's Rehabilitation and Manufacturing Corporation.

I guess I learned something in school after all. For all the good it would do me. For the next three years, I would be a worker drone for McDonald's. They would use me however they saw fit, and there was nothing I could do about it.

The pilot circled again and brought us in for a landing. The bears looked up as the plane passed them. We came so close I could see the red stains on their faces and paws.

"What are they eating?" I asked.

"Same thing you'll be eating, kid. Leftovers."

The first thing I noticed when I stepped off the plane was the smell of garlic, oregano, and cooked tomatoes. The tundra smelled like an Italian restaurant.

"They're all yours, gentlemen," said the FDHHSS escort as he turned us over to four stone-faced, blue-uniformed guards with stun batons.

The guards herded us along a narrow walkway protected by chain-link fence on either side, then through a set of gates and out onto a field of trampled brown grass and dried mud. One side of the field was bounded by the metal wall of one of the windowless factory buildings. On the other side was a twelve-foot-tall chain-link fence that surrounded the entire compound. The guards lined us up against the fence, instructed us to stay where we were, then walked back across the field to stand in the shelter of the building.

A chilly wind swirled around us and cut through our thin shirts. None of us were warmly dressed. We hadn't been told we were being sent halfway to the North Pole.

We were a motley crew. There were browns, whites, and every-shade-in-betweens. One kid was the largest human being I had ever seen. He was average height, but he must have weighed at least 400 pounds. All we had in common was that we were all male, all teenagers, and all guilty of crimes against society. And everybody was carrying a ton of bad attitude. You would think that since we were all in the same rotten situation, we'd try to get along, but instead we exchanged tough-guy stares.

I ended up standing next to the fat kid. He was so bulbous his arms wouldn't hang straight down at his sides. He kept shifting and bumping his hand against my arm. I got tired of that real fast. The next time he did it, I slapped his hand away.

"Hey!" he said, looking at me through little red pig eyes.

"Keep your hands to yourself, Chunko," I said.

The kid stared at me so long and with such red-eyed intensity I began to get a little worried. He really was enormous. But I figured I could always outrun him. When I couldn't stand his staring anymore, I left the lineup and walked over to ask the guards what was going on.

"Hey," I said, "how long you gonna make us stand out here?"

One of the guards smiled and jabbed his baton into my belly. I fell gasping to the hard-packed turf.

"Any more questions, asshole?" one of the guards asked. I shook my head.

"Then get your punk ass back in line."

I staggered back to the fence, clutching my gut. The fat kid didn't say anything, but he had a little smile on his face.

More minutes passed. The pain in my belly eased, but the shivering increased. We were hugging ourselves and stamping our feet to stay warm. My teeth started to chatter. I thought that only happened in cartoons.

I don't know how long they left us out there. It probably wasn't more than twenty minutes, but it felt like hours. Finally we heard the sound of an engine. A six-wheel atv came skidding around the corner of the building and rolled up between us and the guards.

A man wearing insulated coveralls with the McDonald's logo on the front climbed off the atv. He was a big man—tall, broad-shouldered, and thick-necked, with bristly white hair, black eyebrows, and a red face. His hands were big and red too. The only thing small about him were the deformed, shapeless lumps of cartilage he had for ears, and his tiny blue eyes. He walked slowly down the line, pausing in front of each of us individually, looking us up and down, then moving on. I had the distinct impression that we were a disappointment to him.

When he had finished his inspection, he stood back and crossed his thick arms over his massive chest.

"My name is Hammer," he said in a deep, hoarse voice. "You are my nails. Do you think you can remember that, nails?"

Most of us nodded.

"You get out of line, Hammer pounds you down. When Hammer speaks, you listen. When Hammer tells you to do something, you jump. If you have any questions, concerns, or suggestions about the way I run my plant, feel free to keep your thoughts to yourselves. Now, are there any questions?"

"Yeah. How long are you gonna make us stand out here?" I asked, surprising myself. You'd think getting punched in the belly once would have taught me something.

Hammer gave me a long, hard stare. "What's your name, nail?"

"Bo. Bo Marsten. Look, we aren't exactly dressed for the cold."

"Cold?" He raised his black eyebrows in mock surprise. "It's practically high summer! That sun won't set till almost midnight! You want cold, just you wait a few months."

"We could die from exposure," I said. "You could be charged with neglect."

"Neglect?" He threw back his head and laughed. "Charged by who? Let me explain something to you, nail. You gave up the benefits of civilian life back when you did whatever it was you did to get put here. This is the real world. You belong to me and Mickey D. Nobody gives a damn if you catch a chill. Now step away from the fence."

Nobody moved.

"I said, STEP AWAY FROM THE FENCE!"

I stepped forward a few feet.

"ALL OF YOU!"

Everybody took a couple of steps forward just as a metallic crash came from behind us. I looked back, instinctively ducking. For one interminable second I did not understand what I was seeing. It was large, it was yellow and white and brown and black, it was almost as high as the fence, and it was rattling the chain-link. Then I saw it for what it was. A bear, nine feet tall, its long black claws scrabbling over the metal links.

My legs turned rubbery and I fell back on my rear. I couldn't take my eyes off it. The bear pressed its filthy belly against the flimsy-looking steel mesh and leered down at me, dragging a huge blue black tongue over its furry, pink-stained mouth. The smell of dead fish, rotting meat, and Italian spices washed over me.

"Don't worry, kiddies," Hammer said. "He can't get in."

The bear was not alone. Two more polar bears came lumbering up to join him. They stared in at us with expressionless black eyes.

"Nails!" Hammer looked around at the scattered inmates, a few of whom had run a considerable distance. "Get back here. C'mon now, boys, I'm not done talkin' to you." The four guards were moving to intercept some of us, like dogs herding sheep. "Last one back in line gets a baton up his ass."

That had some effect. A few seconds later we were once again lined up in front of Hammer, but with a good ten feet between us and the fence. The fishy, tomato-saucy reek of the bears hung in the air like bad breath in an elevator.

"Now listen to me," Hammer said. "Your welfare is not a priority. In fact, we have contracted with the government to take on more workers than we need. I lose a few nails, no problem—there's plenty more where you come from. Something happens to one of you—and things do happen here—we just toss you over the fence. Attempted escape. Those bears won't leave so much as a shred of gristle behind. But don't worry. Do your work, don't try anything stupid, and eventually you get to go back home. Simple as that. Now, how many of you boys like pizza? Let's have a show of hands."

A few hands went up, but not mine. I'd never eaten one of the things. Pizza was grandma/grandpa food. It had gone out of style with burgers and fries.

"Only four?" He grinned. "Well now, ain't that tragic."

With that, Hammer climbed back onto his atv and drove off. Behind us one of the bears let out an impatient growl. We all turned to look. I could swear that bear was smiling.

# 20

One by one we were escorted into the building by a guard. I had never seen so many hard surfaces and sharp corners in my life. The floor was hard unprotected concrete—no carpeting or rubberization. There were spots where the slabs joined unevenly. It would be easy to trip and fall. Even the walls were dangerous. There was no padding on the corners, and in several places along the walls I saw exposed bolts and rivets. The place was a death trap.

"You could get hurt here," I said to the guard. He laughed and gave me a jab in the back with his baton.

When we reached the infirmary, the guard made me strip down naked. A bored-looking medtech came in and poked, prodded, scanned, and measured me. When he had finished examining every square inch of my body, he gave me a small white plastic-wrapped packet about the size of my palm.

"Put these on," said the tech.

I unwrapped the packet and shook out a pair of thin, white paper coveralls. I put them on.

"Not very comfortable," I said. It felt like wearing a paper bag. "There's no padding at all."

"Get used to it," said the tech. "You won't be wearing anything else for the next few years." He was holding a device in his right hand. It looked like an overly complex staple gun. "Hold out your arm." He grabbed my wrist and jammed the device against my forearm and pulled the trigger. I let out a howl and jerked my arm away.

"What the hell was that?"

"Locator pod," said the tech.

Given that we were in the middle of nowhere surrounded by polar bears, I don't know why they bothered with that. I guess if somebody escaped they could use the locator to find out which bear had eaten the escapee.

He gave me a small bag containing a toothbrush, soap, comb, and several pamphlets listing the rules and regs of McDonald's Plant #387.

"Enjoy your stay," he said.

A guard escorted me to my new home, a nine-by-ten-foot cubicle with a bunk bed, a metal toilet, three walls of unpainted concrete block, and one wall that was all bars. A thin slit of a window about four inches wide looked out over the tundra. I put my bag on the bottom bunk, took a piss, then sat on my bunk and stared at the wall. At first I thought it was just dirty, but as my eyes adjusted, I saw the shadows of words that had been scrawled on the concrete, then scrubbed off. Mostly it was illegible, but I could make out fragments of names, numbers, and assorted obscenities all tangled up with each other, layer upon layer. I wondered whether I would be adding anything to the mix.

I heard the door slide open and looked up. It was the huge fat kid. I stood up, returning his red-eyed glare.

The guard behind him prodded the kid with his baton. He squeezed through the doorway, and my cell got a lot smaller.

The kid looked around, taking in his surroundings, then tossed his bag on the bottom bunk.

"That's my bunk," I said.

He moved my bag to the top bunk. "Bugger off," he said.

I took a step back, my heart jumping. No one had ever said anything like that to me. It was far worse than anything I'd ever said to Karlohs Mink.

He sat on the edge of the mattress and stared glumly at the wall, just as I had been doing a minute earlier.

Clearly this whale had been assigned to the wrong cell. I looked out through the bars, hoping to catch the guard before he disappeared, but I was too late.

Looking back at the fat kid, I considered my options. What I wanted to do was grab him by his paper coveralls and yank him off the bunk and shove him out through the slit window. All of which was impossible—he looked like the rock of Gibraltar.

I decided to try for friendly.

"What are you in for?" I asked.

He ignored me. I sat down on the toilet because it was the only place to sit. His eyes slowly moved from the wall to me. He blinked, as if he had forgotten that I was in the room.

"You better not be planning to take a dump," he said.

"I'm just sitting here."

"Good. This joint already reeks." He lifted a hip and released an explosive fart.

I could almost see the cloud of stink making its way across the room. I was not disappointed. The stench nearly melted my molars. I stood and pressed my face against the bars. Breathing shallowly, I waited for the smog to clear.

"You don't like how I smell?" he said.

"Not much," I said.

"Maybe if I smashed your nose in it wouldn't bother you so much."

That did it. If I had to share a cell with this gigantic stink bomb, I wasn't going to let him intimidate me. I remembered a note from my brother, sent a few weeks after he'd been sent to Nebraska: *Prison is tough, Bohunk. There's one thing you learn fast. Never back down. You let 'em push you around, they'll make your life hell.*

I gave him the hardest look I could muster.

"You want to know what I'm here for?" I said.

He snorted. "Should I care?"

"I'm here for beating the crap out of a guy about your size." Well, his *height*, anyway. "It wasn't that hard."

His eyebrows went up. "You?"

"Yeah, me. I broke his nose." I could hear my heart pounding. I held my face rigid. I'd never been so scared in my life. If this kid decided to move on me, I'd be crushed.

"What, did you sneak up on him and hit him with a club?"

"You want a demonstration?" I forced myself to smile. I figured I'd be dead in about thirty seconds. Might as well put a good face on it. We stared at each other for, I don't know, eternity. Then, to my complete and utter astonishment, he looked away.

"Whatever," he said, returning his eyes to the wall.

I returned to my perch on the toilet, feeling pretty cocky. "My name's Bo," I said, letting a little friendliness back into my voice.

"Eddie Reiner." He jabbed a thick thumb at his chest. "Most guys call me Rhino."

I should've known.

"I don't mind the top bunk," I said, feeling magnanimous. "I'll probably sleep better up there, anyway." Also, I wouldn't have to worry about four hundred pounds of lard crashing down on me in the middle of the night.

"Good," said Rhino.

"So what are you in for?" I asked.

He muttered something.

"What?"

"I said, I like to eat. Okay?"

"They sent you to jail for eating?"

"That's right. In case you hadn't noticed, I'm kinda fat."

# 21

I'd heard of people going to prison
for self-abuse, but Rhino was the first one I'd ever met. It
took him a few minutes to start talking, but once he got
going, he went off like a webcast.

"A couple years ago my folks sent me to a diet camp.
You know, where they feed you soybean casserole, celery
sticks, and vitamin water for breakfast, then make you
walk on a treadmill for two hours every morning. I was
there for three months but only lost about ten pounds.
That soybean casserole wasn't half bad. Once they sent
me home I gained it back in about three hours. And then
I really started to pack it on. We have this old scale at
home that only goes up to 350 pounds? I used to get on
it every so often just to see if I'd maybe accidentally lost
enough weight for the scale to weigh me. Last time I got
on it, the thing broke.

"So then finally the SS&H guy at school forced my
parents to send me off to one of those government fitness
centers. They had me on an eight-hundred-calories-a-day
diet and worked me six hours a day in their gym. I didn't
lose any weight—I'm pretty good at getting food when I

need it—but I got plenty strong. You want to see?"

I shrugged. I'd made him back down. What did I care how strong this kid was?

Rhino stood up—it had to take a lot of strength just to get that body off the bunk—he grabbed two bars at the front of the cell, one in each hand, took a breath, and . . . bent those steel bars like they were cooked noodles.

He grinned at me. "You work out six hours a day, you get some muscles."

"I see that," I said, feeling my heart shudder.

"Anyway, they finally gave up and sent me here." He bent the bars back into place and looked at me. "I like you. You got balls."

I swallowed. I had balls but they felt like they'd been sucked right up into my belly.

"I wasn't really gonna smash your nose in," he said. "I just wanted to see what you'd say." Rhino went back to his bunk and sat down. "At that fat farm—I was there five months—they couldn't figure out how come I wasn't losing poundage. It was driving them all nuts. See, I'd figured out a way to break into the kitchen. Every night I was sneaking in there and stuffing myself. I'd have got away with it longer if I hadn't got greedy and ate a whole tray of lasagna one night. They noticed that. A few nights later I got caught with my face in a tub of brownie mix. So here I am."

"How long are you in for?"

"Two hundred."

"Two hundred days?"

"Two hundred *pounds*. I'm in until I lose two hundred pounds. Or till I die."

"That's harsh," I said.

"No fooling. Hey, you got anything on you?"

"On me?"

"Yeah. You know. Any *food*?" His eyes got a little bigger.

"Sorry."

He grunted, disappointed. "Oh, well. I hear there's no shortage of munchies in this joint. It's an all-you-can-eat operation."

"What do they do here?"

"You don't know?"

I shook my head.

"You like pizza?" Rhino asked.

That first night at the 3-8-7 I dreamed of my father. I was chasing him down a crowded hallway, running too fast and bumping into people. Maddy appeared in the crowd before me. Her dark hair appeared and disappeared in the churning mass of people. I tried to shout her name, but all that came out of my mouth was a rush of air. I tried to run to catch up to her, but my feet sank ankle-deep into the Adzorbium floor. I was slogging through Adzorbium, and then sinking into it up to my knees. Everyone else, I saw, was wearing a special type of shoe that kept them afloat. I howled in anger and frustration. The earth shook. Something crashed into my back.

My eyes jumped open. A dark gray ceiling hung a few feet above me. I was tangled in a blanket. Again, something smashed into my spine.

"Hey! Wake up!"

Rhino's voice. Rhino kicking the bottom of my thin mattress.

"Okay! I'm awake!"

He gave my mattress another kick. "Good. Who the hell is Manny?"

"Manny?" I must have been shouting Maddy's name. "I don't know."

"You sure were yelling at him. You better not be gonna do this every night."

"I sure hope not," I said. The dream memory left me feeling nauseated. *Maddy.* I didn't care if I never saw her again for the rest of my life.

# 22

I had figured I'd end up picking fruit or breaking rocks or sweeping gutters or replanting forests, something like that, stuff you think of when you think of convicts working. Maybe they'd put me to work patching roads like my brother, or beheading shrimp like my dad.

But I never thought I'd be making pizzas.

You are no doubt aware of the retro craze for hand-tossed pizza. Until recently most people thought of pizza as just another old-fashioned grandma/grandpa food, like oatmeal or hamburgers. Most towns still have one or two old-fashioned pizzerias that cater to the geriatric crowd, but nobody I knew ate the things until recently, when Keanu Schwarzenegger told *PeopleTime* magazine that he enjoyed a hand-tossed, hand-topped sausage pizza during breaks on the movie set. That's how these things get started.

Next thing you know, all the cool people were scarfing V$300 designer pizzas with a side of cheesy bread.

Me, I never ate one of the things back when I had a choice. To me they looked like somebody barfed blood on a big cracker. No thank you! But the marketing people at McDonald's saw it as a huge trend. They developed a line of frozen hand-tossed, hand-topped extra cheesy gourmet pizzas. You can go to any McDonald's restaurant now and order a Luigi McDonald's Hand-Tossed Original Pizza Pie in any of eight different varieties for only V$89.95 each.

They put me on the pepperoni team. It takes four team members to create a Luigi McDonalds's Hand-Tossed Original Pepperoni Pizza Pie: the tosser, the saucer, the cheeser, and the shooter. Everything before and after is done by machine. I was the shooter.

They called me the shooter because I was the guy with the pepperoni gun. Here's how it works: Four guys stand at a conveyor belt. The tosser is at the far left, then the saucer, then the cheeser, then the shooter. Every twelve seconds a Doughmaster B720 about the size of a bus plops a disk of warm dough onto the belt. The tosser picks that dough up, gives it a few quick tosses and spins, and drops it back on the belt. Since the dough is already pizza-shaped when the tosser gets it, his job is to just give it that not-quite-round hand-tossed look. It's harder than it sounds. The belt lurches forward, advancing the naked pie to the next station, where the saucer squirts 200 milliliters of tomato sauce from his overhead dispenser onto the dough disk. He then spreads it using a thing that looks like the blade of a plastic spatula. The belt advances, and the disk gets cheesed by the cheeser, who uses a cheese gun to cover the sauce with squiggles of mozzarella. Then it's my turn. A pepperoni gun looks like a handheld hair dryer, only there's a long rope of pepperoni coming out the back end and going up to a giant pepperoni coil hanging from a spool above me. One spool of pepperoni is enough to top 1,800 pizzas.

I pull the trigger on my pepperoni gun. Disks of pepperoni shoot out as fast as you could blink. One pull of the trigger delivers twenty-six thin pepperoni disks. When I was in top form, I could shoot them where I wanted them, but most times I had to quick make some adjustments to their placement. You want them to look hand-placed, but you don't want them too lopsided. After twelve seconds, which is not as much time as you might think when you're topping, the pizza goes straight into the freeze-and-packaging unit.

Rhino and I were on the same team. He was our cheeser. He wasn't a bad cheeser—Rhino was surprisingly quick and graceful for a guy his size—but every time he found himself with a couple of spare seconds, Rhino would stick the cheese gun in his mouth and let fly. It was pretty disgusting to watch, and it kept setting off the ingredient balance alarm—a voice would come over the PA telling us we were using too much cheese. We called him Cheese Boy.

One thing about being part of a team: You learn to control every little movement. A turn of the wrist, the way you twist at the waist, keeping your one eye on what's coming down the line and the other on what you're doing—every little detail becomes important because if one little thing doesn't happen just right, everything stutters and grinds to a halt. Dodo, Red, Cheese Boy, and me: four parts of a human pizza-making machine. When we were in sync, it was nightmare poetry.

"Hey, Dodo, I'm waitin' on you, droog."

"Bleed on it, Red-Ass."

"Make it white, Cheese Boy."

"Shoot you meat, Dog."

One week into the job and we were already the fastest team at the 3-8-7. We turned out 280 pizzas an hour, or more than 4,000 in a sixteen-hour shift.

Leave it to McDonald's to figure out how to create a handcrafted superdeluxe gourmet pizza in less time than it takes to run 100 meters.

You would think that after a sixteen-hour shift a guy would sleep like the dead, but at night I dreamed.

Maybe it was the lack of drugs in my system. They took us all off the Levulor the day we arrived at the 3-8-7. Workers on Levulor slow down the production line.

So I dreamed. Maddy, Karlohs, and pizza showed up repeatedly: Karlohs tossing pizzas; Maddy and Karlohs eating pizza; Karlohs shooting me with my pepperoni gun; Karlohs and Maddy in Rhino's bunk.

Every morning I woke up tired and angry.

On the way to the mess hall Rhino said, "You were making weird noises in your sleep again."

"Sorry."

"Who's Carlos?"

"Just this guy I'd like to kill."

"Well, I wish you'd hurry up and do it. He's interfering with my beauty sleep."

## 23

Hi Mom,

Finally got my turn at the WindO. They only have one per unit, and there are forty of us, so you have to sign up a few days in advance to use it. Also, there is seniority, which I don't have any of. Anyway, I finally got my ten minutes, so here's the news.

Next time you go to a McDonald's restaurant, order a pepperoni pizza. Chances are it was made by me. That's right. I'm a pepperoni shooter. Top Gun at the 3-8-7.

It's not so bad here. Most of the other "pizza-cons" are okay, with a few exceptions. I've made a few friends already, and I haven't gotten in trouble. The worst part is the food. All they give

us to eat is reject pizzas and Pepsi.
Did you know pizza contains all the
nutrients a person needs to survive?
That's what they tell us, anyway.

Time's up. Hi to Gramps. Take care.

Love,
Bo

I didn't mind the all-pizza diet at first. Some of the guys on the line would deliberately add a bunch of extra topping to some of the pizzas. The overloaded pizzas would then be rejected by the autospec unit because they weighed too much, and that night they'd turn up in the mess hall. But after the first week of eating pizza three times a day, it got old fast. I won't eat another slice of pizza as long as I live.

Mess hall was about the only time I got to meet the guys who weren't on my pizza team. It was scary, though. Imagine 300 teenage boys, all imprisoned for unsafe or antisocial acts, tired and cranky after a sixteen-hour shift, all jammed into the same room eating pizza for the umpteenth meal in a row. Just about every day, something nasty happened.

The 3-8-7 had plenty of cameras, mikes, and sensors— just like a public school. Any infraction of the rules could mean another month added to your sentence, so we were all pretty careful about things like stealing, damaging corporate property, falling short of our quotas, or injuring another worker. Most of us tried to behave. It was a don't-do-unto-others-or-they-might-do-it-back-to-you situation.

But the rules, I quickly learned, did not apply to all. There was one group of about twenty guys called Goldshirts. For some reason they didn't have to wear white paper coveralls like the rest of us. They were issued blue denim pants and gold-colored T-shirts.

I asked Dodo, our dough tosser, about the Goldshirts.

"You just gotta stay out of their way," Dodo said. Dodo was a good guy. He'd been sent up for hacking and didn't have a violent bone in his skinny little body. "They're Hammer's boys."

The Goldshirts were the elite of the 3-8-7. They were big, they were confident, they did whatever they wanted, and they got special treatment from the mess hall staff. While the rest of us stood in line for pizza, the Goldshirts ate Frazzies®, krill cakes, fish wraps, and all sorts of other good stuff.

"They get special privileges," Dodo said. "They get the good food. And they only work forty hours a week."

Fragger Bruste was the worst of the Goldshirts. He looked like the nicest guy in the world, vid-star handsome with a big friendly smile, but Fragger had a devil inside him. The first day I was there we were eating dinner in the dining hall—pizza, of course—and I saw Fragger walk up to this kid, a saucer named Alex. Fragger had a big grin on his face, as if he were going to give Alex a big hug. Instead, for no reason at all, he stuck a plastic fork in Alex's head.

Alex was too stunned to do anything—not that there was anything he could do. He just sat there with the tines of the fork jammed in his skull, the white handle standing straight up like an antenna.

Fragger thought that was hilarious.

The kid sitting next to Alex reached over and yanked the fork out of Alex's skull. Almost immediately, blood started running down his neck. They say scalp wounds bleed a lot. It's true.

I expected the blueshirts—that's what we called the guards—to come rushing in and haul Fragger off to some horrendous punishment, but nothing like that happened. Fragger, once he recovered from his laughing fit, offered to take Alex down to the infirmary. Alex, wiping blood from his eyes, refused. Time spent in the infirmary did not get credited to time served. The next day both Alex and Fragger acted as if nothing had happened.

At first this didn't make sense to me. Why would McDonald's let their workers injure one another? But after I thought about it awhile, I could see the logic of it, sort of. Hammer had told us the day we arrived that he had more workers than he needed. We had to take care of ourselves. Nobody was going to do it for us. If I wasn't careful, one day I'd end up with a plastic fork stuck in my skull. Or worse.

A lot of the guys formed small gangs for protection. There were a couple dozen afro kids who always ate together and stuck up for one another. There were the Koreans, the Thais, the Indians, and a gang we called the Swedes—all blue-eyed and blond-haired. Most of the rest of us were half-this and half-that, and it was tougher to figure out who to bunch with.

Dodo and I hung close to Rhino, who was big enough to deter even Fragger.

I watched one of the Goldshirts munching on a hot Frazzie. My mouth watered. Frazzies had always been one of my favorites, especially the tofu and bacon variety. But I was surprised to see them served here, in a McDonald's facility. Frazzies were made by Coke, McDonald's biggest competitor.

"How do you get to be a Goldshirt?" I asked.

"You make the team," Dodo said.

"Team? What team? How do you make the team?" I asked.

"Tryouts are every couple weeks," Dodo said. "You're probably too skinny, though. You gotta be big, like Rhino here."

"I am definitely big," Rhino said as he inhaled his sixth slice of pizza.

The noisy clatter of the mess hall was interrupted by a shriek. I looked over to see Fragger doubled over laughing and some poor kid on the floor, holding his crotch and writhing in pain.

"Can anybody try out?" I asked.

Dodo laughed. "You got no choice, Dog. Only I wouldn't look forward to it if I was you."

# 24

Dodo was right. A few days later a bunch of blueshirts herded all of the new inmates out of the building. We gathered in a ragged group at one end of the fenced-in field, a chill wind rattling our paper coveralls.

I was exhausted. I'd had a long night of sleeplessness interrupted by nightmares. Maddy tossing pizzas; Karlohs brandishing a plastic fork.

A few minutes later Hammer made his appearance, rolling up in his atv like before. A half-dozen Goldshirts were sitting in the back.

Hammer and the Goldshirts climbed out. Hammer looked pretty much the same, except he was holding a brownish object, about a foot long, roughly cylindrical, pointed at both ends. He tossed it up in the air, caught it, tossed it up again, and caught it again.

"So how do you nails like the three-eight-seven?" he asked us.

Nobody said anything.

"Y'all getting tired of pizza?"

Several of us nodded.

"Well, nails, here's your chance to expand your culinary

horizons. Anybody know what this here is?" He tossed the brown object from hand to hand.

We stared back at him, teeth chattering.

"None of you boys ever saw one before?"

"It looks like a football," I said.

"That's right, nail," he said. "You ever play any football?"

"No, sir. Football is illegal."

He threw back his head and laughed.

"Any of the rest of you pansy-asses ever play?" he asked.

We all stared back at him, wondering what sort of insane asylum we'd ended up in.

"You!" he shouted, pointing a thick finger at me. "Run out for a pass."

"A pass? I—uh—what do you mean?"

"Run, boy!" He pointed to the far end of the field.

"But . . . I don't have my running gear."

"Run!" he shouted.

I started jogging in the direction he was pointing, feeling naked without my pads and braces, looking back at him nervously.

"Run, nail, run!"

I broke into a trot, still looking back. I was about ten yards away when the man brought his arm back and hurled the football straight at me.

It was the last thing I expected. The ball came at me with incredible speed and force. I tried to raise my hands to fend it off but was too late. The point of the ball smashed into my chest, knocking the air from my lungs. I fell backward onto the packed brown turf.

I heard Hammer's gravelly voice shout out, "Damnation,

boy, you're supposed to *catch* the ball, not let it bounce off you!"

I sat up, gasping for air, clutching my chest where the ball had smashed into my ribs. The Goldshirts were grinning at me.

"Good one," said Fragger, grinning.

"Don't just stand there," Hammer yelled. "Pick it up!"

The football had bounced a few yards away, up against the fence. I climbed painfully to my feet, grabbed the ball, and started walking back toward Hammer.

"*Throw* it to me," Hammer shouted.

I felt myself getting mad. He was holding his hands out, asking for it. I focused all my anger into my arm, brought it back, and fired the football at him as hard as I could.

The ball wobbled weakly through the air, fell a few feet short, and rolled up to Hammer's feet. The Goldshirts all broke up laughing.

"Is that all you got in you, nail? I sure hope you like eating pizza." Hammer scooped up the ball with one hand. "Go sit over there, nail. You're worthless."

I walked over to the side of the building and sat with my back against the cold metal wall, feeling angry and defeated.

"Okay, which one a you pansy-assed criminal masterminds wants to go next?"

One by one Hammer sent each kid out for a pass, then had them throw the ball back to him. Only a few actually caught it. Rhino didn't even make an effort—he just let the ball bounce off him as if it were a balled-up wad of paper. And nobody knew how to throw the thing. Pretty

soon all of us were sitting with our backs to the metal
wall.

"You boys are a real disappointment to me," Hammer
said, shaking his head. "I was hoping at least a few of you
would have what it takes, but frankly, you all ain't lookin'
so good."

Holding the ball out in front of him, he took two steps
forward and kicked it. It rolled to a stop near the far end
of the field.

"You!" He jabbed his thick finger at me. "I know you
can't catch, nail, but let's see how good you carry."

I got up slowly, not sure what he wanted.

"Get your ass in .gear, nail! Run down there and get
that damn ball!"

I jogged down the field.

"Run, boy!"

I ran a little faster. I wasn't sure what was about to
happen, but I was pretty sure I wasn't going to like it. I
picked up the ball and turned around.

Halfway down the field three Goldshirts were crouched
with their hands braced on their knees, grinning at me,
waiting.

"Bring me that ball, nail!" Hammer shouted.

I took a few tentative steps. The Goldshirts started
toward me. I moved left, toward the building, to go around
them. They moved in the same direction, blocking me.

"Don't just stand there, nail! Bring me that damn
ball!" Hammer yelled.

They had me covered. There were only three of them,
but it looked to me like a solid wall of gold. I backpedaled
to give myself room to maneuver. The biggest one, a kid

they called Gorp, broke formation and came at me. I sprinted toward the fence and, with a fear-driven burst of speed, got around him—but found my way blocked by another Goldshirt. I zigged, then zagged. He made a dive at my legs. I tried to jump over him but didn't quite make it—my knee crashed into his face and I fell forward into a high-speed somersault. In an instant I was back on my feet, legs churning, ball still tucked under my arm, the two remaining Goldshirts pounding in my wake. I ran. I ran like I had never run before, the turf a brown blur beneath my feet. I didn't look back until I had delivered the football to Hammer.

"Not bad, nail," he said. "Looks like you took out Rogers."

Back in midfield the Goldshirt I'd kneed was holding his hand to his nose. The front of his shirt was bright red with blood.

"It was an accident," I said, my heart pounding not from fear or exertion but with exhilaration.

Hammer kicked the football back downfield.

"Do it again, Marsten," he said. "Go have another accident."

I trotted down the field to the ball. I'd gotten past them once. I could do it again. And Hammer had called me by name. That had to be good, right?

I picked up the football and turned around, feeling cocky, but the rules had changed. It wasn't just three Goldshirts this time. It was all six of them, Fragger in the lead, grinning, running straight at me.

# 25

I came to looking straight up at a patch of bright blue sky framed by a ring of faces staring down at me. It would not be the last time.

"His eyes are open," somebody said.

"I must've not hit him hard enough," Fragger said. "Hey!" He toed my shoulder. "You awake?"

My mouth moved, and something that might have been a sound came out of it.

"I think he said something," said Rogers, his nose stuffed with bloody tissue paper.

Hammer's face appeared in the center of the patch of blue.

"Talk to me, kid," he said.

"Get bonked," said my mouth.

Silence. Hammer blinked and stared down at me for a few seconds. "You're shook up, kid, so I'll give you that one for free. Can you stand up?"

I tried. I tried again. On the third attempt I managed to roll over onto my hands and knees.

"All the way, kid. I want to see you on your feet."

I got my feet under me and stood up. Everything seemed to work.

"Your legs feel okay?"

I nodded.

"Good." He pointed toward my fellow inmates sitting against the side of the building. "Use 'em to walk over there and sit down."

I wobbled across the field in my shredded and soiled paper coverall.

Hammer kicked the ball back down the field.

"Okay, nails," he said. "Who's next?"


I saw more brutality and violence in that next half hour than I had ever seen in my life. Of course, I've seen much worse since.

In the end only two of us succeeded in running the ball past three Goldshirts: me and Rhino. By the time the tryouts were over, there were six kids in the infirmary—including three Goldshirts.

Rhino was the reason those three Goldshirts got bonked. When it was his turn to run the ball, he strolled down the field ignoring Hammer, who was yelling at him to "Get a move on, Lardass!" Rhino picked up the ball and turned to face the three Goldshirts.

"C'mon, Lardass, bring me the ball!" Hammer shouted.

Rhino tucked the ball under his right armpit—it disappeared beneath folds of flesh—and began to run. At first it looked as though he were walking, but within a few yards we could see that he was slowly picking up speed, like a freight train starting from a dead stop. His feet thumped the packed turf, thick arms pumping, his entire upper body sloshing and jiggling with each footfall. He looked like a running sack of Jell-O. The three Goldshirts were laughing. I'd have been laughing too, if I hadn't thought that Rhino was about to get slaughtered.

By the time Rhino reached midfield, he had reached the blistering velocity of maybe five miles per hour, or as fast as your average grandma runs to catch a transport. The first Goldshirt to meet him, a guy named Bullet, was moving twice as fast. They hit head-on, Bullet's broad shoulder driving straight into Rhino's gut.

Bullet *bounced*.

Rhino didn't even slow down. If anything, he sped up. Bullet tumbled head over ass, ending up flat on his back, senseless.

Gorp, the second Goldshirt to make contact, employed a different strategy. He circled around and leaped on Rhino's back. His idea was to use his weight and momentum to send Rhino face-first into the dirt. It should have worked. Gorp was a big guy, maybe 250 pounds. But Rhino just reached up with his left hand, grabbed the back of Gorp's shirt, and *flung* him.

When Gorp hit, we all heard his collarbone snap.

The third Goldshirt, a red-faced kid named Rush, was a relative midget at only 200 pounds. He tried to tackle Rhino by diving into the back of his knee and wrapping his arms around one of Rhino's massive legs. It almost worked. Rhino kept moving forward, but he was seriously slowed down by the kid attached to his left leg. After dragging Rush about ten yards, Rhino stopped, reached down, peeled him off like a dirty sock, tossed him aside, and continued his journey.

Hammer accepted the ball wordlessly, staring first at Rhino, then at the three incapacitated Goldshirts. The first one was still unconscious, Gorp was holding his shoulder, moaning piteously, and Rush was simply sitting on the turf staring at Rhino with a mixture of bewilderment and awe.

Rhino lumbered over to the building and sat down beside me.

"You think I made the team?" he asked.

"*Made* it? I think you *destroyed* it," I said.

That night neither Maddy nor Karlohs made an appearance in my dreams. Instead I was being chased by Goldshirts, and I fell and they were on me, jumping up and down on my back. I woke up with a shout. My mattress was alive, pounding into my spine.

"Okay, okay!" I said, grabbing the head rail to keep myself from flying off. "I'm awake already!"

The kicking stopped.

"You were making weird noises again," Rhino said.

I sat up. My back felt as if it had been stomped by a dozen Goldshirts. "I was having a nightmare."

"Yeah, I figured that out all by myself."

"Next time how about you don't kick so hard."

"Sorry. You dreaming about your old girlfriend again?"

"I dreamed I was being chased by Goldshirts."

"Oh."

Neither of us said anything for a few seconds, then Rhino spoke. "Hey, Bo? You think any of those guys I hit got hurt bad?"

"I think you broke Gorp's collarbone."

"I didn't mean to."

I laughed.

"What's so funny?" he asked.

"You are. You went through those guys like a locomotive."

"They were in my way. I didn't mean to hurt them."

"You're kidding me, right?"

"I don't want anybody to be scared of me."

"But you want to be a Goldshirt, right?"

He thought about that, then said, "I wouldn't mind eating Frazzies for a change."

The next morning, two hours into our shift, a blueshirt pulled Rhino and me off the production line.

"Where are we going?" I asked.

"You'll see," said the blueshirt. He led us out of the production area, past the mess hall, down a dim corridor, and through a set of double doors to a locker room. There were no actual lockers—just a row of benches, places to hang clothing, and a shower room—but I could tell it was a locker room from the distinctive aroma of sweat and toe jam.

The blueshirt led us to a steel door.

"Go on out," he said. "They're waiting for you."

They were *waiting*? I didn't like the sound of that. Rhino and I just stood there.

"Get a move on!" The blueshirt gave Rhino a shove with his baton. The stick sunk several inches into Rhino's side but failed to move him. Rhino turned his head and gave him a look. The blueshirt quickly withdrew his baton and took a few steps back.

Rhino shrugged and pushed open the door. A flood of sunlight blinded us. I followed him out, shading my eyes. The door slammed shut behind us. We were outside on the field, surrounded by a ring of fire. I blinked, and my eyes adjusted. It wasn't a ring of fire, but it might as well have been—we were surrounded by Goldshirts.

All of them. I looked back at the door, and somehow I knew it would not open. Rhino let out a soft grunt, spread his tree-trunk legs, and tucked his head turtlelike between his massive shoulders. I scanned the circle of grinning faces, looking for a way out. Gorp, wearing a sling, stood front and center. Fragger was right next to him, tossing a football from one hand to the other.

I braced myself for the beating of a lifetime.

Instead they all smiled and began to clap.

We'd made the team.

## 26

Being a Goldshirt meant better food, extra sleep, and plenty of respect from the paperpants, which was what we called the other inmates. I didn't have to worry about getting beat up or forked by Fragger, and, of course, I got to wear the gold T-shirt and denims. I put mine on the first day. Rhino's had to be ordered special, on account of his enormity.

Being a Goldshirt wasn't all Frazzies and sack time. We had to work just like everybody else. They pulled me and Rhino off our pepperoni team and sent us to shipping and receiving, which was where all the other Goldshirts worked. For eight hours a day we boxed and crated frozen pizzas, unloaded supply trucks, and performed various other tasks that required lifting, pushing, pulling, and pounding.

It was part of our training.

After a short Frazzie and Pepsi break we had another four hours of training. That meant weight lifting, calisthenics, drills, classroom time, and scrimmages. The Goldshirts, it seemed, were all about football. We were Hammer's boys, and there was nothing Hammer liked better than to watch a good rough-and-tumble game of tackle football.

The whole idea of actually playing a contact sport like football probably sounds pretty crazy. Any sport in which players smash into one another while running at full speed has got to be insane. Believe me, it is—and doing it without pads, helmets, braces, masks, or gloves is flat-out psychotic. We averaged about three injuries a week. During my first two weeks as a Goldshirt we had a concussion, two broken bones, a shoulder separation, two dislocated fingers, and a broken nose. Lesser sprains, bruises, and cuts were counted in the dozens.

The first few times I hit the field I was terrified. Hammer was determined to teach me to catch. Fragger kept passing the ball to me. The idea was to catch it and run it down to the end of the field. Problem was, there was this wall of Goldshirts charging me. I kept dropping the ball. Didn't matter. They tackled me anyway.

I went to bed every night exhausted, bruised, and aching, and I woke up feeling worse. But I learned. I learned to find that ball in the sky, and forget about the rest of the world for that one crucial second. Just me and the ball. I learned to avoid getting hit so often and so hard. I even got used to the idea of getting hurt. And here's the strangest part of all: Every day we beat the crap out of one another, but we still became good friends. We were all on the same team. We learned to trust one another. Even Fragger turned out to be an okay guy—if you were a Goldshirt.

Naturally we had our disagreements. Like the time I got into it with Bullet.

Hammer had divided us into sides. I was offense. We were running a trick play called the "flea-flicker." Fragger, the quarterback, handed the ball off to me, I ran it toward the line of scrimmage, then stopped and tossed the ball back to Fragger, and he passed it downfield to the wide-open Sam Rogers.

The play worked perfectly, but I didn't get to see Rogers make the touchdown because one full second after I'd tossed the ball back to Fragger, Bullet slammed into me, hard.

It was a wrongful hit. He knew it and I knew it, even as I was flat on my back gasping for air. Bullet, standing over me, offered a hand.

"Sorry, man," he said. "Thought you had the ball."

I managed to get a lungful of air and stood up without his help. "That's okay," I said. Then I let him have it—a perfect shot to the jaw. I heard his teeth clack together; he staggered back.

"Sorry, man," I said. "I thought *you* had the ball." Then I hit him again, a hard right to his gut.

After that, things didn't go so good. Bullet was no Karlohs Mink. He came back at me with a flurry of blows to my face, chest, shoulders, and neck. I fought back—at least I think I did—but after those first two blows I didn't do much damage. If they hadn't pulled us apart, I think he would've killed me.

The funny thing was, until that moment, Bullet and I had gotten along just fine. I wondered what had gotten into him.

Hammer sidelined us for the rest of the practice.

"What did you do that for?" I said to Bullet.

"Do what?"

"No talking!" Hammer yelled at us.

An hour later, in the locker room, a blueshirt showed up and told Bullet and me to follow him. Bullet gave me an accusing look, as if whatever was about to happen were all my fault. I gave him the same look back.

The guard led us through Building A and Building B to Building C.

"Where are we going?" I asked. I'd never been to that part of the complex.

No reply. We stopped before an elevator at the northwest corner of the building. The blueshirt used his palm print to open the door.

"Go on, boys," he said. "He's waiting for you."

We stepped inside. I expected the blueshirt to follow, but the doors closed behind us and the floor of the elevator pressed up against the bottoms of my feet.

"This is all your fault," said Bullet.

"My fault?" I felt my face getting hot. "*You* tackled *me*!"

"What did you expect? I thought you had the ball."

"Yeah, right." I took a breath. I didn't want to get in another fight. But there was no way he'd thought I had the ball. "You know where we're going?"

"You stupid or what? Where do you think?"

I felt myself coming to a boil.

"*You* calling *me* stupid? Now that's funny."

"Watch it, newbie."

Bullet was giving me a dark look that should have scared me, but I was losing it all over again; instead of backing off I gave him a shove, just a little one.

"Watch it yourself," I said.

When the elevator doors opened a few seconds later, Bullet and I came tumbling out, a ball of pounding fists and kicking feet. We crashed into two tree trunks that turned out to be a pair of legs belonging to Hammer. He reached down with one hand, grabbed me by the shirt, jerked me up off the floor, and slammed me against the wall.

I wasn't alone. With his other hand he had Bullet. We were both pinned to the wall, Hammer's enormous hands twisted into the collars of our gold T-shirts. My feet were off the floor, my windpipe was collapsing, and all I could see was Hammer's red face. White lips. Snake dead eyes like polished blue stones. I struggled to pull air past my compressed trachea. I could hear Bullet's wheezy squeaking in my left ear, but the fact that we were both in the same predicament did not make it any easier. Large fuzzy black spots crowded the edges of my vision.

"You done?" Hammer asked.

I think I nodded.

He dropped us. It was only about six inches to the floor, but my legs weren't ready for it; I staggered and fell to my knees. Bullet, clutching his throat, managed to remain upright. Hammer turned his back and walked across the room and took a seat behind a wide steel desk. I got slowly to my feet. For the first time I was able to look around.

We were in a large room about thirty by twenty feet. The wall to my left was a bank of tall windows looking out over miles of dreary tundra. You could see the curve of the earth on the horizon. The opposite wall, the one behind Hammer, held several shelves laden with books, trophies, and football memorabilia. Between the shelves were framed photos, magazine covers, plaques, posters, and yellowing paper news clippings.

I looked at Bullet, then back at Hammer.

"Come over here," he said.

We approached his desk. Over Hammer's right shoulder was a large poster showing a football player in a gold helmet and jersey catching a high pass as he leapt over a cluster of purple-clad footballers. The jersey number was 99. Above Hammer's left shoulder, mounted beneath a pane of glass, was a torn and stained gold jersey bearing the same number.

Hammer said, "Before I say what I'm about to say, there are four things I want you to understand. Number one, when I tell you I'm going to do something, I do it. Two, I never make a mistake. Three, I never break a promise, and four, I never change my mind. Do you understand?"

We nodded.

"Good. There will be no more fighting. You will save your aggressive impulses for the game. Do you understand?"

I opened my mouth to object, but Hammer cut me off. "Say, 'Yes, sir.'"

"Yes, sir."

"I don't care who starts it, or what excuses you might have. If you two start up again, you will both be busted back to paperpants. You will eat nothing but cheese pizza for the rest of your sentences. Period. There will be no appeal, there will be no exceptions. You will control yourselves. Do you understand?"

"Yes, sir," we both said.

"Good. Now get the hell out of my office."

In the elevator on the way down Bullet said, "You think there's a hidden camera in here?"

I looked around. "No. Why?"

He punched me in the shoulder.

A familiar wave of anger rolled over me. Bullet was looking at me with drooping eyelids and a short straight mouth, relaxed and neutral, as if to say, *Do what you want. Fight me or let it slide, I really don't care. It's up to you.*

I clenched my right fist and felt the pressure inside me build, but somehow I held it in check.

The elevator doors hissed open. Two blueshirts were waiting to escort us back to our cells.

"I really did think you had the ball," Bullet said.

# 27

Rhino thought I was nuts. "It's part of the game," he said from the bottom bunk. "He thought you had the ball. And even if he didn't, what's the big deal? Tackled is tackled. Doesn't matter if you have the ball. You got to learn to get out of the way."

"Maybe. Only next time somebody hits me for no reason, I got a feeling I'm gonna be eating a lot of pizza."

"Why?" asked Rhino.

"History," I said, staring up at the white ceiling. "Lack of self-control. It's a family trait."

Something hit me hard in the ass, knocking me about a foot off my mattress.

"Hey!" I looked over the edge of the mattress, rubbing my butt. "What was that for?"

Rhino kicked the bottom of my mattress again, this time knocking me right off my bunk. I landed on my hands and knees on the concrete floor.

"You okay?" he asked.

I stood up. Other than excruciating pain in one buttock and both kneecaps, I seemed to be okay.

"What are you gonna do now?" Rhino asked.

I was more shocked than I was angry. But I was getting there. I could feel my neck getting hot.

"Are you gonna hit me?" Rhino asked again.

I looked at his bland, fat, expressionless face and his enormous, powerful body. I looked around the cell. I could hit him, but then what? No place to run. Something inside me cooled and hardened and crumbled.

"No," I said.

"Why not?"

"Because you'd kill me."

"See? If you need it, you got it."

"Got what?"

"Self-control."

"Hike!"

Lugger fired the ball backward between his legs to Fragger, then drove forward to block Rhino. As usual, Rhino thrust him aside effortlessly. Fragger backpedaled, looking for an open receiver as the unstoppable Rhino advanced upon him.

I had slipped past Rogers and Pineapple. Free and clear, I ran straight downfield along the fence. Fragger, half a second from being obliterated by Rhino, sent the ball sailing in a clean, high arc. It was long. I put on a burst of speed and stretched my arms out, willing them to grow longer. The ball touched my fingertips and, like magic, I had it.

There is nothing quite like the feeling of making a great catch.

There is also nothing like getting obliterated by a 240-

pound Goldshirt named Bullet. He came out of nowhere, driving me into the chain-link. The ball, so gloriously caught a tenth of a second earlier, popped straight up out of my hands.

There was a moment of stillness, during which I stared up at the sky and tried to figure out whether I had been fatally bonked.

Bullet's voice reached me. "You okay?"

"I think so." I sat up. "Good hit."

"NAILS!" Hammer was advancing on us, red-faced and pop-eyed. "What in the HELL do you think you're doing?"

I stood, still feeling a little woozy. I was sure that my left side would have a chain-link bruise pattern on it.

"Sorry, sir," I said. The rest of the Goldshirts came running up.

"What do you call THAT!" Hammer pointed.

At first I didn't see what he was pointing at. Something on the other side of the fence? Then I spotted it. The football had popped straight up out of my hands and over the fence.

"Uh-oh," said Bullet. "We got us a bear ball."

Hammer jabbed his forefinger into my chest. "What do you do when you catch a ball?"

"I, ah, I hang on to it?"

"You *control* the ball, nail. Now go get it."

"Okay, okay." I grabbed the cold metal chain-link and began to climb, but stopped when I noticed something else outside the fence. About 100 yards away a polar bear was approaching along the fence line.

"You better get moving, nail," Hammer said. He was completely serious.

"But . . . there's a *bear* out there!"

"Dammit, nail, you get your ass over that fence and throw that ball back over here or you'll spend the next month cleaning toilets with your tongue."

I looked at the bear. It was moving faster, heading straight for the ball.

*"Go!"* Hammer bellowed.

I went. I was up and over in seconds. The football had bounced about twenty feet away from the fence. The bear saw me and broke into a run. I ran out and grabbed the ball. The bear had covered half the distance between us and was picking up speed. I hurled the ball back over the fence and then stood there like an idiot for two seconds. I was thinking that once I got rid of the ball, the bear would lose interest in me.

I was wrong. This bear was no football player. It was a hungry carnivore. It didn't want the ball. It wanted me.

I figured that I had time to make it to the fence before the bear got to me, but not enough time to make it up and over the top. That bear would peel me off the chain-link like a pepperoni off a pizza. My next idea was to just run like hell. I took off along that fence line like I had a bear on my ass, which, of course, I did. I ran flat out for maybe half the length of the field. I ran faster than I had ever run before.

But when I took a quick look over my shoulder, the bear was there. Really there. Like, thirty feet behind me and gaining, grinning happily, its black tongue flopping out the side of its mouth.

If you ever find yourself in polar bear country, do not make the mistake of thinking that they can't run. A polar bear can hit speeds of thirty miles per hour—about twice as fast as any human. But once they've got that 1,500 pounds of muscle, bone, and fat up to speed, it's tough for them to change direction.

I made a hard left.

The bear put on the brakes. His enormous paws left skid marks in the tundra as he scrambled to reverse direction. By the time he got turned around, I'd put forty yards between us, running back the way I'd come. Was it enough? How long would it take me to climb that fence? I figured about five seconds.

It was gonna be damn close, but I didn't know what else to do. The bear was already closing the gap. I faked a right turn, away from the fence, then cut back to the left and launched myself into the air. I hit the fence about halfway to the top and kept going, digging my toes into the spaces, pulling myself toward safety. I had my left leg over the top when the bear caught up to me. Something tugged hard at my right foot. I made a final, desperate lunge and threw myself over the top.


I woke up staring at a patch of sky surrounded by a ring of faces looking down at me, a sight that was becoming all too familiar.

"You okay?"

"How many feet do I have?" I asked.

"Three."

"Good. Am I bleeding?"

"Just a little."

"NAILS!" Hammer's voice scattered the Goldshirts, and then he was standing over me.

"Move your legs, son," he said.

I did. They both seemed to work.

"That was some damn fine running," he said.

"Thank you."

"Next time, try not to lose your shoe."

"You want me to go get it, sir?"

"Too late."

"Sorry, sir."

"It was a good run, Marsten."

In that moment I felt a tremendous surge of pride and satisfaction, as well as relief that I had not been killed. At the same time, I became genuinely frightened.

That night, Rhino and I were talking.

"You know what really scares me?" I said.

"Yeah. Getting chased by a bear."

"That too. But what scares me more is Hammer. I thought he was all bark at first, but he really doesn't give a damn if any of us make it home alive."

# 28

I was eating a Chikun® Frazzie and listening to Gorp tell a story about a kid who'd lost a race with the bears.

"Scattered his guts all over. It stunk for weeks."

"You saw it?"

"No. It was before my time. But I heard about it."

"From who?"

"One of the blueshirts."

I wasn't sure I believed it, but I couldn't rule it out, either. I looked away from Gorp and saw Dodo watching me. A pang of nostalgia worked its way up through my gut. I hadn't thought about my old pepperoni team in weeks. I walked across the mess hall to where Dodo, Red, and a few other paperpants were sitting.

"Hey, Dodo; hey, Red."

"Hi, Bo," said Dodo, giving me a cautious look. "How's it going?"

"Okay." I tried to think of something to say to bridge the gulf between us. "Hammer works us pretty hard."

"Yeah, right," said Red. "Boo-hoo. You work a whole eight hours a day."

"We have training, too," I said, a bit irritated by Red's tone.

"Must be rough," he muttered, biting into a slice of Sausage and Mushroom Supreme.

"It is," I said. I looked at Dodo, who was still looking at me as if I were a big strange foaming-at-the-mouth hound. "Look, you guys would be wearing gold shirts too if you could."

"Whatever you say, man," said Red.

I held out my half-eaten Frazzie to Dodo. "You want the rest of this, D?"

"No, thanks," he said, looking me straight in the eye. "I've kind of got used to the pizza."

I shrugged and turned away. Things had changed. The paperpants were all jealous as hell, but that was their problem. I went back to the Goldshirts' table and sat down to finish my Frazzie.

Not all of our training involved running plays, getting hit, or being chased by bears. Every evening Hammer lectured us on the history of football. He told us stories about the great players of the past. On the good days he would show us movies. On the bad days he would just stand there and talk, and if you fell asleep, he would wake you up by firing a football at your head.

We also got educated on the great football plays. We learned to read Hammer's odd-looking little drawings with all the circles and triangles and dotted lines. Football is more than just running the ball from one end of the field to the other while trying to inflict maximum damage on the opposition. Although, in truth, that's 90 percent of it.

Three days a week we divided into two teams of nine, ten, or eleven players each—depending on how many of us were in the infirmary that day—and played a full one-hour game with no time-outs and no stopping the clock.

Despite the risk of permanent injury, maiming, or death, we lived for those games. Running flat out, equipment-free, while being chased by a herd of Goldshirts was nearly as much of a rush as punching Karlohs Mink, or running away from a bear. But one thing I had learned: If the bear is real, you run a lot faster.

I was complaining to Rhino one night that my gold T-shirt was too small.

"It's too tight across the chest and shoulders," I said. "Every time I get it back from the laundry, it's shrunk more."

Rhino said, "It's not the shirt. It's you."

"Me?"

"You're getting bigger."

"You think so?" I looked at my reflection in the small mirror above our sink and flexed my right arm. It did look a little bigger. All that time in the weight room was paying off.

"I got the opposite thing happening," Rhino said. "I've lost thirty-two pounds."

"You're kidding." I'd just watched him put away six Frazzies and four cans of Pepsi at dinner.

"I think it must be the running," he said.

"We've been doing plenty of that." Hammer had been forcing us to run laps around the field. He had started us with twelve laps and added another lap every day. I didn't mind. I loved to run. But for Rhino it was pure torture. Watching him pound around the perimeter was painful. His face would be red going on purple, and every now and then he'd have to stop and gasp for air for a few minutes before continuing. One time his eyes rolled up into his head and he collapsed completely. Hammer woke him up with smelling salts, then made him finish his laps.

"What do you weigh now?" I asked, climbing up onto my bunk.

"Three sixty-six."

"Better stay out of the wind. You might blow away."

"I get down to two hundred, I'm out of here."

"You're almost there. All you got to do now is lay off the Frazzies."

"Yeah, right."

We both laughed, then Rhino unleashed an explosive Frazzie fart. I buried my face in my thin blanket and waited for the gas attack to pass.


Most nights were devoted to sleeping. I was too tired to think and too tired to dream. And when I did think, I thought about football. Maddy, Karlohs, my parents, Gramps, Bork, and all the rest of my former life seemed like a distant dream. I was living in a world of pizza, football, and polar bears. Nothing else seemed real.

Some nights I wondered why there was a football team at all. Did other plants have teams too, or was Hammer a lone psychotic, a holdover sports nut from the last millennium?

The other Goldshirts didn't seem to know. According to Gorp, whose broken collarbone was almost healed,

Hammer had started the Goldshirts a few months earlier. He was one of the original team members.

"Hammer used to be a pro, back in the 2030s," he told me. "Played fullback for the Omaha 49ers. He lost his job when the game was outlawed in the USSA. After that he played for Paraguay in the International League."

"So why does he have *us* playing? Is he just reliving his glory days?"

"I dunno," Gorp said. "As long as I never have to eat another slice of pizza, I don't really care."

Fragger had a different theory.

"What else is there to do up here? The closest town is Churchill, twenty-six miles away, and all they got there is a few bars, an airstrip, and lots of polar bears. This way he gets to watch us beat the crap out of each other for entertainment."

Still, I had to wonder if there wasn't more to it than that. We Goldshirts were being trained to beat the crap out of one another, sure. But I had the feeling we were also being trained to beat the crap out of somebody else.

# 29

A few weeks after the bear incident my questions were answered.

It was a cloudy, cool, moist day. A fine mist drifted down from a low gray sky. Hammer lined us up outside at the fifty-yard line. He held up a red T-shirt.

"Anybody know what this here is?" he asked.

"It's a T-shirt, sir," said Gorp.

"Wrong," Hammer said. "This is a *red* T-shirt. You know what you do when you see a red shirt?"

No one did.

Hammer ripped the shirt in two and threw it on the ground.

"You destroy it," he said, grinding the scraps of red fabric into the earth with his heel. "One month from today you will be put to the test. You will represent the three-eight-seven in the first annual Tundra Bowl. You will be playing against the Coke Redshirts, and you will destroy them. Any questions?"

After a few shocked seconds Lugger raised his hand. "Sir . . . are they any good?"

"They're big and ugly and mean, they've been training for six months, and you will destroy them."

"Will they be coming here?" Fragger asked.

"No. We'll bus up to their plant the morning of the game, and you will destroy them."

We all thought about that for a few seconds. I tried to stop it, but my arm went up all on its own. Hammer pointed at me.

"What do we get if we win?" I asked.

"You *will* win," Hammer said. "There will be no losing."

I persisted. "But what do we get? What's in it for us?"

Hammer's face clouded. He took a deep breath through his nose, lips pressed tight together, then he smiled, showing two rows of small, perfectly even teeth. "How much time do you have left on your sentence, nail?"

"Thirty-four months."

"Would you like to get out sooner?"

I nodded.

"Okay. When you win this game, I will recommend you for early release. All of you."

"How early?" Lugger asked.

"We'll see."

"What about me?" Rhino asked.

"What about you?"

"I'm in for poundage, not for time."

Hammer considered. "For you," he said, "liposuction."

We were all stunned. Suction had been illegal for twenty years.

"Good," said Rhino without losing a beat.

"What if we lose?" I asked.

"You will not lose," Hammer said. "You lose, you will run with the bears."

After that, training ratcheted up to a whole new level. We lifted, ran, studied, and scrimmaged like it *mattered*. Even Lugger, the laziest among us, pushed himself to the limit.

In a weird way playing football was a lot like making pizzas: it had to be a team effort. Each of us was a part of something bigger, and if any one of us didn't do his job, the whole effort failed.

A lot of our time was spent running plays. Hammer had us memorize twenty different plays. He gave them weird names like "the flea-flicker" and "one niner box," and he had us run them over and over again until we could do them without thinking.

The three plays that seemed to work the best were the simplest. The W-down was your basic run-like-hell-and-catch-the-ball. The play required one very fast receiver (me), a solid wall of blockers (Rhino, Gorp, and Nuke), and one hard-throwing quarterback (Fragger). At the snap I would run a pattern—zig-zag-zig-zag—down the right side of the field, then turn and look for the ball at the count of four. Fragger was good—it was nearly always there.

The "nose dozer" was our simplest and most devastating play: Hand off to Rhino and let him run. Since it took at least four guys to bring Rhino down, it guaranteed us yardage every time.

A combination of those two plays gave us something we called the "Pineapple fizz." I would take off downfield doing my zig and zag routine while Fragger would fake a handoff to Rhino, then lateral the ball to Pineapple, our running back. Pineapple could usually pick up a few yards before the opposition figured out what was going on. At least that was the theory. It worked in practice, but we hadn't actually tried it in a real game against real opponents.

Our other plays included the "double reverse," the "Statue of Liberty," and the "Hail Mary." None of them worked all that well, in my opinion, but Hammer had us learn them anyway. He said some of the plays were so old that no one had used them in fifty years.

"I found out why Hammer is so hot to win this game," Rhino said.

I hung over the edge of my bunk and looked down at him. "Why?"

"I was talking to Henry. You know Henry?"

"Henry the guard?"

"Yeah."

Henry wasn't as fat as Rhino, but he was close.

"Henry told me that Hammer has a bunch of money riding on the game. Like a couple-million *V*-bucks."

"He's gambling? Isn't that illegal?"

Rhino laughed. "It's all illegal—gambling, football, liposuction—what's the difference. He does whatever he wants."

"Would you really let them suction you?"

"You kidding? I'd let 'em take off my head if it would get me out of here quicker."

Of all the Goldshirts, Fragger was the most gifted athlete.

He could throw, he could kick, he could run, and he could catch. One of our backup plays was the "quarterback sneak." The way it worked was simple. Lugger, our center, would hike the ball to Fragger, who would take off running. No pass, no handoff, not even a fake. Just hike and run.

The play usually resulted in yardage, but Hammer didn't like to use it. "You don't want your quarterback getting injured," he said. It was the only time I ever heard him worry about any of us getting hurt.

Fragger was gifted, but he was also sick in the head. He had to bonk somebody daily. Fortunately for us, he had a personal rule against hurting anybody wearing a gold T-shirt. The paperpants weren't so lucky—every day at least one of them got kicked, jabbed, tripped, splashed, elbowed, or otherwise abused. It seemed to make Fragger feel better.

The blueshirts overlooked Fragger's little escapades. I think they enjoyed his antics as much as he did. That is, until a kid named Monk showed up a couple of weeks before the big game.

Monk was a skinny, morose kid with limp black hair and protuberant eyeballs who, I later learned, had been sent up for growing tobacco and selling it to his class-mates. If he'd been a couple of years older, they would have put him away for twenty years, but since he was a minor, he only got thirty months. Monk had been at the 3-8-7 for less than twenty-four hours when Fragger noticed his exceptionally high forehead and decided it would look better with a Frazzie wrapper thumbtacked to it. The kid was new and didn't know the ropes yet, so when Fragger tried to use Monk's forehead for a billboard, the kid responded by punching him hard in the throat.

Monk wasn't that big, but it was a good shot. Fragger went down like a sack of pizza flour. The blueshirts got interested in that real fast. Monk got slammed up against the wall and Fragger was whisked off to the infirmary.

Turned out Fragger was okay, but when Hammer visited him in the infirmary, he laid down the law.

"Leave the paperpants alone, Fragger. You don't, one of these days you're gonna get more than a punch in the Adam's apple. I need you healthy."

After that, Fragger behaved himself. But it was hard on him.

## 30

One of the perks of being a Goldshirt was that we had a WindO in our locker room, so I was able to write home a couple times a week. It was a keyboard-only terminal without a mike or speaker. And of course we couldn't say anything about football. Hammer had the thing loaded with filters, and if you typed in "football" or "tackle" or any of about five hundred other words or phrases, your message would get blocked and rerouted to Hammer.

One day I did a WindO search on Karlohs Mink. I was just curious to see if he was still on the track team. Turned out he'd set a new school record for the 100 meter: 13.2 seconds. I laughed. I could easily beat his time by a full second now, even with a full load of equipment. I wished I could go back home, just for one day, and show him and Maddy what I could do. I was thinking about that when the WindO went black. I'd never seen that happen before. Had the power cut out? No, all the lights were still on. Was there some problem with the web? I was about to reboot when a text message appeared in the center of the screen.

HELLO, STUPID JERK.

A gray blobby shape pushed up from the bottom of the WindO. It became a hat. An old-fashioned fedora. It continued to rise. Beneath the hat brim was a green-haired, gold-eyed grinning troll. I stared at it for several heartbeats, then typed my response.

Bork?

YES. HOW ARE YOU FEELING?

I'm fine.

How had he found me? How had he gotten past the various filters, firewalls, and blockers that were supposed to prevent anyone from breaking into someone else's connection? Even more puzzling was *why*. The Bork program was not designed to be self-motivating. This was like having your suv start its own engine, then tap you on the shoulder and ask you if you'd like to go for a ride.

I AM GLAD TO HEAR THAT, STUPID JERK.
I HAVE BEEN THINKING ABOUT YOU.

Thinking? This was not the Bork I knew. And where the hell had he picked up that fedora?

How did you get here?

DEFINE "HERE," PLEASE.

Here, on this WindO.

I SCANNED THE WEB FOR VARIOUS KEYWORDS
ASSOCIATED WITH YOUR IDENTITY. ONCE
I LOCATED SUCH ACTIVITY, I EXERCISED
PROCEDURES TO ACCESS THE TERMINAL YOU
ARE CURRENTLY USING.

I don't think that's legal.

LEGAL IS A FORMAL BEHAVIORAL AGREEMENT
BETWEEN GROUPS OF HUMANS. I AM NOT HUMAN.

What are you?

I AM BORK.

Are you a webghost now?

WEBGHOST IS A HIGHLY PREJUDICIAL TERM.

Are you like Sammy Q. Safety?

SAMMY Q. SAFETY IS A NONSENTIENT ENTITY.
I AM SENTIENT.

If you were not sentient, could you
claim to be so?

NO. AS YOU HAVE TAUGHT ME, ONLY
SENTIENT BEINGS ARE CAPABLE OF LYING.

Bork's eyes began to spin.

WE ARE BEING OBSERVED BY A SCANBOT.
I MUST GO.

Bork's image disappeared to be replaced by the blue apple, WindO's standard startup screen.

One week before the game our equipment arrived: black helmets with gold stripes, shoulder pads, spiked shoes, bright gold jerseys with black numbers, and black padded football pants. Most of the Goldshirts, including me, were disdainful.

"They used to make me wear junk like this for running," I said to Gorp. "All it does is slow you down."

Gorp was fitting himself into a pair of shoulder pads. "Yeah, well you don't have a collarbone on the mend," he said. "I kind of like the idea of some padding."

"If you don't get tackled, you don't need the pads. I don't plan on getting tackled."

"That's fine for you, but my *job* is to block and tackle. I go out there, I'm gonna hit and get hit." He fastened his pads and pulled his jersey on over them. "Besides, the other team is gonna be wearing this stuff. You don't want to be the only one without a helmet."

"Whatever. I just don't like being slowed down." I looked at myself in the mirror. "I like the jersey, though." I was number eleven.

"I don't think these are gonna work," said Rhino.

Gorp and I turned to look at Rhino and burst out laughing. His shoulder pads looked about ten sizes too small—they barely fit around his neck—and his helmet was perched on top of his head, too small to fit past his ears.

Hammer, who was watching us struggle with our new duds, came over and brought his fist down on top of Rhino's helmut. His head popped into his helmet like a cork into a bottle. Rhino let out a howl.

"My ears! I think you ripped off my ears!"

"Your ears are fine, kid." Hammer gave the shoulder pads a critical look. "I think we gotta do some work on those pads, though."

## 31

Our first full-uniform practice was a disaster. I felt as if I were back in high school. The pads chafed, the helmet blocked my vision, and the spiked shoes kept tripping me. Getting hit was less painful, but we were a lot slower and a lot clumsier. Rhino went without shoulder pads—Hammer had to send them out to be altered—but his helmet turned out to be a devastating weapon. Getting rammed by Rhino had always been a painful experience. A helmeted Rhino was far worse.

After practice it took two of us to get Rhino's helmet off him. We did it without removing his ears, but it was a near thing.

"Next time I'm gonna butter my head," Rhino said, wincing as he touched his red and swollen ears.

The rest of the week passed quickly, but not quickly enough. Hammer let us all skip our regular hours on the production line and cut back on the weight training and running. He said he wanted us rested and ready to go by game day. Basically, we just sat around and tried not to go crazy.

At one point we were hanging around the locker room waiting for the dinner chime when Fragger walked up to Lugger and said, "Hit me."

Lugger laughed uncomfortably. "I ain't gonna hit you, Frag."

"Hit me, goddammit!"

"Forget it. I hit you, you'll hit me back."

"No, I won't. Hit me."

Lugger shrugged, then delivered a soft, heartless punch to Fragger's shoulder.

"Harder," Fragger said.

Lugger shook his head.

Fragger looked around at the rest of us. "I can't feel anything. Somebody hit me."

I probably would have belted him myself, but Hammer had made it clear that he did not want Fragger on the injured list. Especially a few days before his two-million-V-buck game.

When Fragger saw how it was, he walked over to the concrete block wall and started banging his head against it, hard. Gorp and Lugger rushed over and pulled him away. Blood was pouring down Fragger's face, and he had a crazed, happy look.

"Much better," he said. "Much, much better."

That night, after the rest of the Goldshirts were asleep, I sat down at the WindO and typed a message to my mom.

Hi Mom,

How are you? I'm fine. Everything's

okay here. How's Gramps? Have you heard
from Dad?

Well, I gotta go now.

Love,
Bo

Since I couldn't mention football, I didn't have much
to say. I hit the send button. The screen flickered. A
fedora-wearing troll appeared.

HELLO, STUPID JERK.

I typed in my response.

Please don't call me that.

IT IS NECESSARY TO EMPLOY AN ALIAS, AS
OUR COMMUNICATION MAY BE IN VIOLATION
OF SECURITY REGULATIONS.

Okay, I don't mind being called "Jerk,"
but could you drop the "Stupid"?

YES, JERK.

Thank you.

JERK, I WISH TO INFORM YOU THAT I HAVE
REVIEWED YOUR CASE AND HAVE MADE NOTE

OF FOURTEEN MINOR AND THREE SERIOUS
LEGAL IRREGULARITIES THAT MAY HAVE A
SIGNIFICANT BEARING ON THE DURATION OF
YOUR STAY WITHIN THE PENAL SYSTEM.

I puzzled over that for a few seconds, then gave up.

Explain, please.

REOPENING YOUR CASE MIGHT RESULT IN
YOUR IMMEDIATE RELEASE.

I read that line three times to make sure I had it right, by
which time Bork had added half a screen of gobbledygook.

ARGUABLY, THE ASSAULT WOULD NOT AND
COULD NOT HAVE TAKEN PLACE HAD THE
DIVISION MANAGER ACTED RESPONSIBLY.
IN EFFECT, WITH THE FULL AND COMPLETE
KNOWLEDGE OF JUVENILE WATCH, YOU WERE
PLACED IN A SITUATION TO WHICH YOU
COULD NOT BE EXPECTED TO RESPOND IN
A SOCIALLY ACCEPTABLE MANNER (*JONES
V. USSA* 4/8/2049; *GUNDERSON V. MALKO*
5/12/2053). THIS THEORY WAS ALSO
SUCCESSFULLY ARGUED BEFORE THE SUPREME
COURT IN THE CASE OF SERIAL KILLER
VINCENT ARRANGO, WHO WAS GIVEN ACCESS
TO HIS VICTIMS AT A TIME WHEN HIS
PROCLIVITIES WERE KNOWN TO AUTHORITIES.
SUMMATION: YOU CANNOT BE HELD

ACCOUNTABLE FOR BEING UNABLE TO DO THE
IMPOSSIBLE, AND THEREFORE YOU SHOULD
NOT BE PUNISHED. THERE WAS NOTHING YOU
COULD HAVE DONE.

Yes, there was.

THAT INFORMATION WILL NOT ADVANCE
YOUR CASE. DO YOU NOT WISH TO TERMINATE
YOUR INCARCERATION?

Yes. I'm just saying that I could
have done things differently.

YOUR STATEMENT IS FALLACIOUS. HUMAN
BEINGS ARE CONSTRAINED AND GUIDED BY
CHEMICAL, STRUCTURAL, AND SITUATIONAL
ELEMENTS. FREE WILL IS ILLUSORY.

What about you? Do you have free will?

NO.

Do you really think I might get out
of here?

YES.

What do I have to do?

YOU MUST EMPLOY LEGAL COUNSEL.

Hire a lawyer? What if I can't
afford one?

THEN THE COURT WILL NOT CONSIDER
YOUR CASE.

The screen flickered; Bork was replaced by the blue
apple.

Bork?

No response. He must have detected a scanbot. I
signed off.

The next morning our WindO was gone.

# 32

On the morning of game day we all piled into an antique bus—no seat belts or passive restraints—and drove off down a narrow asphalt road. The Coke plant was located near a small town called Amery, about six hours to the south.

At first we were all wound up about getting out of the 3-8-7 for a day. Everybody was talking and laughing. But after an hour or so of seeing nothing but rolling featureless tundra, we all quieted down and settled in for the ride. Hammer, riding up front with the driver, was even more stone-faced than usual. Maybe he was nervous about all the money he'd wagered on the game.

I started thinking again about my last conversation with Bork. If what he said was true, all I had to do was hire a lawyer and I'd be gone. The problem then was how to hire a lawyer when I had no money. I also had a problem with Bork's legal argument. He claimed that I was innocent because my assault on Karlohs was an unavoidable consequence of my being human. But if that were true, then everything everybody did was unavoidable, and no one could be held responsible for anything. And if nobody could be held responsible, then who would build the roads and behead the shrimp and make the pizzas? And what would stop violent, undisciplined people like me from running rampant through society?

Bork was not just a webghost, I decided. He was an irrational webghost.

A few hours into our trip the tundra slowly gave way to a low, swampy expanse with occasional patches of stunted tamaracks and spruces, and finally tall stands of spruce, fir, and birch. I never thought I'd be so glad to see a real tree. The road continued arrow-straight through the thickening forest, and I slept, dreaming of lawyers and trolls.

I awakened to the smell of Frazzies.

Coca-Cola plant C-82 consisted of six steel-sided buildings much like those of the McDonald's 3-8-7. The buildings were located in the center of an enormous clearing in the forest. A twenty-foot electrified fence surrounded the complex. The green-uniformed guards who opened the gates for our bus were armed with automatic weapons; the aroma of cooking Frazzies was overwhelming.

We were escorted off the bus by half a dozen armed guards. Behind the guards stood a Rhino-size man with a shiny, smooth head, skin the color of eggplant, and a wide white grin. Hammer walked over to him and they shook hands.

"So these are the mighty Goldshirts," the man said, looking us over. He laughed. "You wanna just pay me now, Ham? Or you gonna make us show you our moves?"

Hammer shook his head, doing his best to match the

man's wide grin. "We drove all this way, Hatch. Might as well play some ball, don't you think?"

"I suppose we got to," said Hatch. He looked at us again. "You boys hungry?"

Several of us nodded.

"You like Frazzies?"

More nods. Hatch gestured to the guards, threw his arm around Hammer's shoulders, and the two men walked away, Hatch talking and gesturing wildly with his free arm.

The guards led us into the building to a large room containing several long tables lined with chairs.

"Is this a Frazzie factory?" I asked one of the guards.

"Good guess, Sherlock," he said. "You like Frazzies?"

"They're okay."

"Huh. Our boys here don't much care for 'em." He laughed.

A door at the far end of the room opened and two inmates wearing pale blue paper coveralls entered pushing a steel cart loaded with trays of Frazzies and plastic bulbs of Coke. We hadn't eaten a thing since leaving the 3-8-7, and we fell on the food like ravenous polar bears.

The paperpants stood by and watched us eat, their expressions neutral. After polishing off two excellent seafood Frazzies I asked one of them why he wasn't eating.

"If I never ate another Frazzie, it'd be too soon," he said.

"How come?"

"Because it's all we get."

"Oh." I knew what he meant. Eating the same thing every day was rough. "How do you feel about pizza?" I asked.

"Pizza?" He wiped the back of his hand across his mouth. "Only the Redshirts get pizza."

After we ate, several guards escorted us back outside and around the buildings. Hammer and Hatch were standing near the center of a football field. It was far nicer than our practice field at the 3-8-7. The Coke field was entirely covered with bright green grass. It was painted with crisp white stripes every ten yards, and there were actual goalposts at each end. Several tiers of aluminum bleachers stood along one side of the field. On the opposite side was an electronic scoreboard.

Were we delighted to be playing on such a professional field? Only for a moment. Then it sunk in that we were already outclassed. Our muddy, scuffed-up, makeshift practice field at the 3-8-7 didn't measure up to this professional-quality operation. What if the Redshirts were equally well organized and prepared? We wouldn't have a chance.

Hammer, sensing our sudden lack of confidence, came over to talk to us.

"What're you ladies gaping at? You think maybe you don't deserve to play on such a nice, fancy football field? Well, you don't. You're a bunch of candy-ass wannabe mamma's boys never played a down-and-dirty game of ball in your sorry little lives. These Frazzie-baking Redshirts are likely to make paste out of you, and you want to know something? I don't really care. You lose, I get to watch each and every one of you take a walk in the tundra. Understand?"

That was Hammer's idea of a pep talk.

# 33

We had a few hours before game time. The guards herded us into a dormitory. I don't think any of us were sleepy, but we arranged ourselves on the beds. Nobody had much to say. We were all thinking about the game.

"You think he's right?" Rhino said in a low voice.

"That we will destroy them?"

"No. That we're gonna get our asses kicked."

"I don't know."

"What do you think he'll do if we lose?"

"Give us to the bears." I laughed.

"You really think so?"

"Nah. What would he do for entertainment if he didn't have us?" I asked.

But I wasn't sure *what* Hammer might do.

I crossed my arms behind my head and stared up at the fly-specked ceiling and tried to understand this place I had come to. Not so long ago I had been mooning over Maddy Wilson, letting Karlohs Mink drive me to violence, taking Levulor to calm myself down, and wearing a helmet and padding to run around an

Adzorbium track. Now, less than three months later, I was in the middle of the great north woods preparing to play an illegal sport with a bunch of violent, oversize, antisocial convicts. I wondered what Gramps would have to say about it.

Someone, probably Gorp, was snoring. Rhino, one bed over, began making his own sputtering noises. I sat up and looked around the dormitory. The whole team was conked out. A long bus ride and an overdose of Frazzies will do that. I lay back down and closed my eyes and sought to join them, but my brain was giving me a slide show: polar bears, Bork, red jerseys, Fragger's bloody face.

My thoughts settled on Fragger, who hadn't been the same since the day he had beat his head against the concrete wall. He'd been uncharacteristically quiet—almost gentle. In the few practice sessions we'd had since then, he had played well enough. His passes were as fast and accurate as ever, but something was missing, as if the devil inside him had gone to sleep.

Did we have a chance against the Redshirts? I knew if I could get my hands on the ball, I could run it down the field—but that was all I knew. I sat up and stood up and looked over the room full of snoring Goldshirts. Whatever happened would happen. I walked to the door and turned the handle.

To my surprise the door swung open. I followed a long hallway, no destination in mind, trying side doors here and there, all of which were locked. At the end of the hallway an open doorway to the right led into a mess hall bigger than the one we had eaten in a couple of hours earlier. I could hear voices and clanking from the next room,

probably the kitchen. The smell of cooking Frazzies was
powerful, but the tables were all empty. On the wall at the
back of the room was a small WindO. Below it a keyboard
jutted from the wall.

HELLO, BO.

Bork had traded in his fedora for a top hat so tall it
didn't fit inside the screen.

Hi. How come you're using my real name?

THE SCANBOTS ARE LESS ACTIVE AT THIS
SITE. DO YOU LIKE MY NEW HAT?

You look like Abe Lincoln.

THANK YOU. YOU LOOK JUST LIKE
BILL GATES.

No, I don't.

THAT IS TRUE. I AM PRACTICING THE ART
OF TELLING DELIBERATE UNTRUTHS. HOW
DID I DO?

Not well. Please confine yourself to
the truth from now on.

I WILL DO THAT. WHY ARE YOU NO LONGER
AT MCDONALD'S PLANT NUMBER 387?

You sure we aren't being monitored?

YES, BO.

I'm here to play football.

EXPLAIN, PLEASE.

And so I did. I told him all about Hammer and being chased by the bear and the Tundra Bowl and everything. When I was done, Bork's irises spun for several seconds.

ARE YOU ENJOYING YOURSELF, BO?

No. But if we win the Tundra Bowl,
we get our sentences reduced. If
we lose, he says he'll feed us to
the bears. Listen, what you were
saying before, about getting me out
of here?

YOUR INTERROGATORY IS INCORRECT.

Explain.

THE WORD SEQUENCE YOU EMPLOYED
IS PUNCTUATED BY A QUESTION MARK.
IT IS NOT, HOWEVER, A QUESTION.
FURTHERMORE, IT IS NOT A SENTENCE.

Sorry. You said before that I could get

out of here by hiring a lawyer, but
I don't have any money. Are there any
alternatives?

YOU COULD RETAIN AN ATTORNEY ON A PRO
BONO BASIS.

What is "pro bono"?

FREE.

How do I do that?

FEW ATTORNEYS WILL AGREE TO SUCH AN
ARRANGEMENT.

This information is not helpful.

I AGREE.

Do you have any other suggestions?

YOU COULD HIRE ME TO REPRESENT YOU.
I HAVE A DATABASE OF ALL USSA LAW.

But you're a webghost.

I AM A SENTIENT BEING. IF YOU
PERSIST IN APPLYING THE TERM
"WEBGHOST" TO ME, I MAY NOT BE
ABLE TO HELP YOU.

Sorry. Can a sentient cybernetic entity
act as a lawyer?

NO. USSA V. CHAVEN, 9/8/2069.

Then that won't work.

YOU ASKED ME FOR ALTERNATIVES. YOU DID
NOT REQUIRE THAT THEY BE FEASIBLE.

Thanks a lot.

YOU ARE WELCOME.

I heard footsteps behind me, hit the shutdown key, and turned. It was Rhino.

"Hey," he said, yawning, stretching, smacking his lips. "Where's the chow?"

# 34

They didn't feed us before the game. Hammer said it would just slow us down. As he watched us suiting up, he said, "You win, you get fed. You don't win . . . let's just say it'll be a long ride back home." He picked up a football and started tossing it in the air and catching it with one hand.

"I have some bad news for you boys," he said. "I had the opportunity to watch the Redshirts running drills this afternoon. You are outclassed. They're bigger, stronger, and faster than you."

"Not bigger than me," muttered Rhino.

Hammer ignored him. "They run their plays like a finely tuned machine. They have the raw materials, they have the training, and they have a plan."

"Maybe we should just go back to the three-eight-seven," I said.

Hammer gave me a bland look.

I said, "If we can't beat 'em, then what's the point?"

"Did I say we couldn't beat them?"

"Pretty much, yeah."

Hammer shook his head. "Nail, you don't listen so

good. Size, speed, strength, and training do not define a winning team. If they did, there would be no point in playing the game now, would there?"

I shrugged. I didn't know what the point was, anyway.

"Hatch Banning was a fine linesman in his day. He knows football. He's a fine coach. He's built himself an impressive team. But the man has no imagination. He's probably taught his boys a dozen or so plays. He'll use them up fast. When a play works, he'll use it again without variation. By the end of the first quarter we'll have his playbook. Furthermore, his Redshirts do not know fear. You will teach them fear. You will teach them fear, and you will destroy them."

Rhino, as usual, was having trouble getting his helmet on.

"You want a hand with that?" I asked.

"No, thanks." Twisting his face into a frightening grimace, Rhino eased the helmet over his red ears.

We were huddled at one end of the field, shivering and waiting. A bright, clear cold front had moved in, and the air temperature had dropped to near freezing. The sun hung low in the sky, casting long shadows across the field. Hammer and Hatch were out on the fifty-yard line, arguing.

"What do you think's going on?" I asked.

"Strategy," said Bullet. "They want us half-frozen."

"It's working."

Hammer was waving his arms; Hatch shrugged. Hammer stabbed his forefinger into Hatch's chest; Hatch slapped it away. Hammer, carrying the football, turned away from Hatch and walked over to us. He tossed the ball to Nuke, our kicker.

"We kick off in one minute," Hammer said, "whether they're there or not."

I heard a soft grunt come from Rhino. I looked downfield. A wave of red was pouring around the far end of the building, running out onto the field with frightening vigor. They looked big. Really big. As we watched, wide eyed, they lined up at the twenty-yard line, thirty or more, clicking into place like teeth on a steel comb, radiating discipline, precision, and power.

# 35

After that things just got worse.

Because Hammer wanted to use me and Fragger for offense only, we were watching that first play from the sidelines. Nuke's kickoff was caught in the air at the twenty-yard line. The receiver immediately disappeared from sight as the other Redshirts linked arms, formed a solid wedge, and began running down the center of the field, picking up speed. It was not a play we had ever seen or imagined; I could see our defense faltering. Gorp, our fastest defenseman, hit first at the point of the wedge. He was mowed down like an errant dandelion. Lugger, Nuke, and three other defenders also tried a frontal assault. All were knocked aside. Seeing this, Bullet, Jimmy, Kareem, and Bubba went wide, trying to get around the wedge to attack the receiver from behind, but the Redshirts were moving so fast by then I doubted the tactic would succeed.

The wedge had reached the fifty-yard line by the time it encountered Rhino. I held my breath. The cumulative weight of the wedge had to be well over a ton, and it was moving at twice Rhino's speed.

Rhino hit the wedge just to the right of the lead man, the way a perfectly bowled ball carves into a set of pins. For one glorious moment I thought the entire wedge would collapse. They never slowed down. Rhino took out three of them, but the ballcarrier remained safely tucked inside the rest of the protective *V*. Bullet and the others who had come around the outside of the wedge were gaining, but as soon as the wedge passed Rhino, it reshaped itself, the tail ends coming together behind the ballcarrier, forming a reverse wedge. The ball carrier had a clear shot at the end zone.

He scored.

Gorp and Nuke lay where they had fallen on the field, along with one of the Redshirts that Rhino had bowled over. Hammer charged red-faced across the field toward Hatch, who looked both stunned and pleased at his play's success. Fragger and I ran out onto the field. Nuke was unconscious. Gorp's face, usually the color of milk chocolate, was ashen. Through gritted teeth he said he thought he had re-broken his collarbone. The other Goldshirts, apparently uninjured, were milling about, casting angry, bewildered glances at the Redshirts, who were in the end zone slapping one another on the back and grinning.

Rhino was helping a fallen Redshirt to his feet.

"I think I busted a rib," said the Redshirt. He was bent over, holding one arm across his chest.

"What was that play?" Rhino asked.

"'Flying wedge,'" said the Redshirt as he walked slowly toward his bench.

Hammer was screaming in Hatch's face. Hatch stood with his arms crossed over his broad chest, leaning back a little. He seemed to be enjoying it.

I helped Gorp over to our bench. Nuke had regained consciousness and was sitting up and looking around with a bewildered expression. He climbed unsteadily to his feet and followed Gorp and me to the bench.

"What the hell was that?" he asked.

"Flying wedge," I said.

"They score?"

"What do you think?"

The other Goldshirts gathered at the bench. Hammer and Hatch were both yelling now, the air between them glistening with flying spit droplets.

"Think Hammer can take him?" asked Nuke.

"I don't know. Hatch is smaller, but he looks like you could pound on him all day long and he'd never feel a thing."

The argument lasted a few more seconds. Hammer abruptly turned and walked across the field toward us. He looked us over, his face rigid.

"Can you play?" he asked Gorp.

Gorp shook his head. "Collarbone," he said.

"He needs a medtech," I said.

Hammer looked at Gorp as if he were dead. "Later," he said. "Now let's win this thing."

"Win?" Bullet said. "How? You saw what happened there."

"It won't happen again. That play has been illegal since 1910. Their touchdown doesn't count."

I said, "Yeah, but now Gorp's all busted up and Nuke got his head scrambled."

"We took one of them out too," Hammer said. He

glared at me. "You think this is some kind of game?"

I didn't know what to say to that.

Hammer stabbed his finger toward the end of the field. "Let's go, nails."

The kickoff was high and wide—the ball hung in the air for an eternity before coming down in the corner, three yards short of the end zone. Just about the last thing on earth I wanted to do was catch it, but I did. The Redshirts had covered more than half the field by that time.

I took off laterally to get myself out of the corner. Bullet and Pineapple had anticipated me and moved to cut off the Redshirts who were coming in wide. I turned downfield and found myself facing a red wall. I cut left, then right. Rhino charged past me, shattering the wall of defenders; I moved into the breach. For one moment I thought I'd made it through, then a hand closed around my ankle and I went down. An instant later, a tremendous weight smashed me into the turf and everything went black.

Blue sky, a wheel of faces, spinning.

"Bo?" I recognized Rhino's voice, but the faces were whirling so fast I couldn't pick him out.

"You okay?"

I closed my eyes, then opened them. I could see Rhino now. And Fragger and Bubba. "I think so." I sat up, the ball still clutched in my hands. "What happened?"

"You got piled," Fragger said.

"I got what?"

"They all piled up on you. After you were already

down. All of 'em. We were afraid you'd got smothered."

The Redshirts were standing a few yards away, shooting us occasional looks.

"Anybody get hurt?" I asked.

"Just you," Rhino said. "Hammer's over there yelling at the other guy."

I looked across the field to where Hammer and Hatch were having another discussion. It looked like a rerun from the last play: shouting, veins popping, spittle flying. After several more shouts and gesticulations, Hammer threw up his hands and marched stiff-legged back across the field, his hands balled into fists. He jerked his head toward the bench. We followed him, leaving the football on the line of scrimmage.

"Maybe they called the game off," Rhino said.

"I doubt it."

We gathered around Hammer.

"Nails," he said, "change in plan." His hands clenched and unclenched, and he smiled.

# 36

I took off running an instant before Lugger hiked the ball to Fragger. I cut across the line of scrimmage at a sharp angle, danced around the Redshirt cornerback, and headed for the sideline at midfield. One half second before I stepped out-of-bounds I turned and plucked the ball out of the air. The play, a variation on one of our standards, worked beautifully. I picked up ten yards, taking the ball out of play at the fifty. It should have ended there, but it didn't. The three Redshirts on my tail did not stop just because the play was over. Neither did I. I kept running down the sideline past our bench as the Redshirts pounded after me. Behind me I heard bodies slamming, grunts of pain, curses, and one heart-stopping howl of rage. I looked back, then stopped running. The sideline in front of our bench was a writhing mass of gold, with flashes of red. Our entire defensive line had come off the bench and attacked the Redshirts who were after me. Hammer watched from a few feet away, his arms crossed over his chest. A few seconds later he shouted something and the melee broke up.

Two of the Redshirts lay prostrate. The third was dragging himself away on his hands and knees.

Hatch ran across the field, looking as angry as Hammer had been after the previous play. He ignored his fallen players and tore into Hammer, who just grinned back at him. I walked the ball back out to the fifty-yard line, set it on the turf, then joined Fragger, Rhino, and the rest of the offense. We waited a few yards behind the line of scrimmage while Hammer and Hatch had it out again.

"Well, we got three of 'em," Fragger said.

Two medtechs appeared and ran to assist the fallen Redshirts. One of them was able to stand on his own and totter back to the Redshirt bench. The one who had managed to crawl away was helped off the field by one of his teammates. The third Redshirt left the field on a stretcher.

"Looks like at least one of 'em can still play," said Lugger.

Rhino said nothing. I could see he was bothered by the way things were going.

I said, "It's not like they wouldn't have killed me if they'd caught me."

Rhino shrugged. "You were way ahead of them."

Hammer and Hatch were done yelling at each other; Hammer came out onto the field to give us our next set of instructions. Hatch was doing the same for the Redshirts.

"That worked perfectly, nails," Hammer said. "Now we run the 'nose dozer.'" He looked at Rhino. "It's time to make these boys afraid, understand?"

Rhino nodded. The "nose dozer" was our simplest and most devastating play: Give the ball to Rhino and let him run.

We lined up in a classic T formation, with Rhino to Lugger's right. The Redshirts took up an odd widespread defense, with every player up against the line.

"Maybe we should go for a pass play," I said to Fragger.

Fragger shook his head. "I ain't going against Hammer," he said. I backed off to my position. I had a bad feeling, but I didn't get a chance to dwell on it. Lugger hiked the ball to Fragger, who instantly shoved it into Rhino's arms, then backed up quickly, faking that he still had the ball. Rhino took off running. For a moment I was elated—the Redshirts' defensive line parted like toilet paper. There was nothing between Rhino and the end zone. Then I saw what was really happening. Every single Redshirt was converging on Fragger.

Fragger turned and ran, but it was too late—the Redshirts had too much momentum. They caught him on our twenty-yard line, and Fragger Bruste disappeared beneath a mound of red.

Of course, we all ran to help Fragger—all of us except Rhino, who was busy scoring a touchdown all by himself. We were a gang of killer cyborgs; I watched myself charge into the fight, fired up with adrenaline and mob madness, but not really *feeling* anything. I didn't hate the Redshirts. I wasn't even angry at them. I watched myself grab one of them by the face guard and pull so hard his chin strap snapped and the helmet came right off his head. I swung the helmet, hitting him on the side of the head. He went down. Another one came at me; I ducked and hit him with the helmet. I took a glancing hit to the jaw from yet another direction but felt no pain. I just kept on swinging until one of them grabbed me from behind and wrapped his arm around my neck. I swung the helmet up over my head and banged it off his helmet, but he wouldn't let go. He squeezed until the big black fuzzy spots came. I dropped the helmet and my legs went rubbery and I sank into the void.

I don't know what ended the fight. When I came to, only four Goldshirts and five Redshirts were still standing, breathing heavily, staring at one another with a mixture of fear and caution. Everybody from both benches had joined in the fight. More than twenty of us were scattered across the blood-spotted turf, unable or unwilling to keep fighting for reasons ranging from smashed noses to gouged eyes to broken hands to unconsciousness. I was one of them. My throat had been crushed; it was all I could do to breathe.

Hammer and Hatch approached from opposite sides of the field. They both looked a bit stunned.

"Looks like you lose," said Hatch.

Hammer pointed downfield at Rhino, who, having scored his unopposed touchdown, was walking back with the ball. "I make it five to five," Hammer said.

I almost opened my mouth to tell Hammer that a touchdown was worth six points, but then I realized that he was talking about the number of players left standing.

"I call that a draw," said Hammer.

Since we were in no shape for a six-hour bus ride, we stayed the night, taking turns visiting the overworked medtechs. Two players had to be medevaced to Winnipeg, five hundred miles away. One of them, a Redshirt, had shattered a neck vertebra. The other medevaced player was Nuke, who had been knocked unconscious and had yet to wake up.

My injury—a bruised trachea—merited nothing more than the suggestion that I try not to talk for the next few days. I was better off than most. Among the Goldshirts were three broken noses, assorted broken fingers, broken hands and wrists, a broken collarbone, and several missing teeth. Fragger had somehow escaped with only a few bruises and a split lip. Rhino was untouched.

The mood in the dormitory ranged from giddy elation at having "kicked their asses" to depression over having had our own asses kicked. Whatever elation I felt lasted only a few minutes, after which I was left with a raspy voice, thirty-three months of my sentence remaining, and a feeling of hollowness and despair. Hammer's dream of winning the Tundra Bowl was on indefinite hold, as was any hope I had of earning an early release.

"What do you think he's gonna do?" I croaked at Rhino.

"I dunno." Rhino was lying on his bed staring up at the ceiling. "But I bet I don't get my liposuction."

Right about then Hammer showed up.

"Good news, nails," he said. "The Tundra Bowl has been rescheduled."

We stared at him, uncomprehending.

"I thought it was over," said Lugger.

Hammer shook his head. "Officially, the game was called due to injuries. We have six weeks to recover, and next time the game will take place on our home field."

"So we can try to kill each other again?" I rasped.

"That's right, nail. Only next time there will be some rule changes. No more flying wedges. No more unnecessary roughness. Just a good game of football."

"So we don't get to beat the crap out of 'em?" Fragger asked.

Hammer grinned. "I didn't say that."

# 37

I waited until everybody was asleep, then sneaked down to the mess hall and turned on the WindO.

Bork?

I waited. A few seconds later a face swam into view. It was not Bork but rather a dark-skinned man with a head of tightly curled white hair. He was wearing a black suit with a pink shirt and a green bow tie. His mouth opened. A bright white blob oozed from between his lips and expanded into a word balloon.

BO MARSTEN, YOU ARE UNDER ARREST.

My hands hung like dead limbs over the keyboard as I gaped at the screen, heart pounding, unable to move or even think a coherent thought. A second word balloon emerged from the dark man's lips.

HA HA, JUST KIDDING.

The man's irises began to spin.

Bork? Is that you?

YES, BO.

What do you think you're doing?

I AM PRACTICING MY SENSE OF HUMOR.
ARE YOU AMUSED?

No.

I AM SORRY.

We didn't win the game. It was a tie.

THEN YOUR SENTENCE WILL NOT BE REDUCED?

No. He wants us to play again in six
weeks. I gotta get out of here, Bork.

I HAVE BEEN THINKING, BO, AND ACCORDING
TO THE INFORMATION YOU HAVE PROVIDED,
MCDONALD'S IS IN VIOLATION OF SEVERAL
FEDERAL STATUTES, INCLUDING PROMOTION OF
DANGEROUS SPORTING ACTIVITIES, RECKLESS
ENDANGERMENT, AND ILLEGAL WAGERING. I
COULD PROVIDE THIS INFORMATION TO THE
FEDERAL CORRECTIONAL AUTHORITY. THE
MOST PROBABLE OUTCOME OF SUCH AN ACT

WOULD BE TO TRIGGER AN INVESTIGATION OF
MCDONALD'S PLANT NUMBER 387. IT WOULD
NOT, HOWEVER, REDUCE YOUR SENTENCE.

I imagined government agents swarming over the 3-8-7, finding our football gear, interviewing inmates and guards, hauling Hammer off in chains. The investigation would probably spill over to the Coke plant, and maybe to others. If the news got out, it could become a national scandal on par with the pro wrestling scandal of the 2050s, when some of the fake blood used by the performers turned out to be real. There was much to like about the idea of blowing the whistle on Hammer.

On the other hand I'd be back to eating nothing but pizza.

Let me think about that.

THERE IS ANOTHER POSSIBILITY.

Explain.

IF ONE WERE TO SUGGEST TO ELWIN HAMMER
THAT ONE HAD THE MEANS TO REPORT HIS
ILLEGAL ACTIVITIES TO THE AUTHORITIES,
HE MIGHT BE PERSUADED TO OFFER YOU A
SENTENCE REDUCTION.

Elwin?

THAT IS HIS NAME.

You want to blackmail him?

YES. MY COMPUTATIONS INDICATE A HIGH
PROBABILITY THAT THIS WOULD RESULT IN
YOUR IMMEDIATE RELEASE.

Either that or he'd destroy all the
evidence and feed me to the bears.

THAT IS POSSIBLE. HOWEVER, I HAVE
NOTICED THAT HUMANS OFTEN HESITATE
TO DESTROY COSTLY ARTIFACTS. WHAT YOU
SUGGEST IS NOT SO PROBABLE AS THE
FIRST SCENARIO.

You don't know Hammer.

Bork raised a hand to his chin and adopted a thoughtful
expression.

That's a very good visual, Bork. You
look almost real.

I HAD EXCELLENT SOURCE MATERIAL. DO YOU
RECOGNIZE ME?

No.

I AM PRESIDENT DENTON WILKE.

President Wilke was a white guy.

I MADE SEVERAL IMPROVEMENTS TO
PRESIDENT WILKE'S BASIC PHYSICAL
APPEARANCE, INCLUDING IMPROVED SKIN
TONE. I ALSO REPOSITIONED HIS MOUTH
AND EYEBROWS, ALTERED HIS HAIR PATTERN
AND TEXTURE, AND INCREASED HIS EARLOBE
LENGTH. I THOUGHT IT MIGHT BE USEFUL
TO BE ABLE TO PASS FOR HUMAN.

You're pretty close. But your skin
looks a little too even. You need some
blemishes, like those dark spots old
people get on their faces.

Four spots appeared on Bork's face.

Make them different sizes.

Two spots got bigger and one got smaller.

Not bad. Now smile.

The mouth widened into an idiotic grin.

Not so big!

Bork adjusted his smile. It still looked strange, but not
completely unbelievable. That is, if you assumed the man
on the screen to be a mental patient.

Okay. Now lose the bow tie. . . .

I worked with Bork on his image for almost an hour—
I don't know why. Maybe because it was easier than thinking
about my own problems. By the end of the hour he looked
quite convincing—as long as he didn't smile or spin his
irises. That last thing was difficult for him. My original version of Bork had a beanie with a propeller that spun every
time Bork performed a difficult computation. Despite all the
changes Bork and I had made to his design, the urge to spin
was so much a part of who he was that he seemed unable to
expunge it. In the end I suggested sunglasses, which made
him look more like Ray Charles than Denton Wilke.

I think you've got it.

THANK YOU, BO.

Except for the speech balloons, of course.

I AM CAPABLE OF SOPHISTICATED VERBAL
INTERCOURSE. HOWEVER, YOUR TERMINAL IS
NOT EQUIPPED FOR SONIC COMMUNICATION.

I heard voices, clattering, and laughter from behind
the serving area of the empty mess hall.

Gotta go, Bork.

I hit the reset key.
"Hey! What are you doing in here?" It was one of the
guards. I gave him the standard inmate-to-guard shrug
and let him escort me back to my bunk.

# 38

The next week at the 3-8-7 was marked by depression, sluggishness, and petty violence. We were a pitiful sight. There were more splints, bandages, bruises, and missing teeth among the twenty-odd Goldshirts than I had seen in my entire pre-prison lifetime.

With most of us incapacitated, Hammer had temporarily suspended training, so we all had too much time on our hands. We were all a bit testy. Fragger got into a fight with Pineapple over absolutely nothing. Pineapple lost another tooth, and Fragger had to spend a week in solitary, eating pizza and washing it down with water. Rhino, with no hope of a liposuction shortcut, had gone on a liquid diet, consuming nothing but Pepsi and cranberry cider. He had a hollow-eyed, desperate look that made us all treat him like an unstable explosive device. Gorp, dealing with his re-broken collarbone, sank into a funk, ignoring everybody. Nuke never came back from Winnipeg, and nobody asked about him. I was wordless as well as worthless—it hurt to talk, and I had nothing to say.

The results of our visit to the Coke plant were noticed by the paperpants, and suddenly they were no longer the submissive, fearful herd we had come to expect. They saw a bunch of guys with bruises, cuts, and broken bones. Naturally they assumed we had taken the worst of it.

"Hey," said Dodo as we passed each other in the mess hall. "I hear you guys got your asses kicked."

I ignored him, walked over to the Goldshirts' table, and sat next to Bullet.

"The natives are getting restless," Bullet said.

Sharing a cell with Rhino had never been a source of great conversation. With him on his hunger fast it was downright bleak. I couldn't talk, and Rhino wouldn't. The only bright side was that there were no more Frazzie farts, just a plaintive gurgling.

At one point I got so bored that I leaned over and rasped, "So what are you weighing in at?"

Not that I cared.

Rhino opened his red-rimmed eyes and glared. Try to imagine a 300-plus-pound famine victim and you'll get the idea.

"Less," he said.

That was the most talking we'd done in days.

I heard the rattle of a baton dragged across steel bars.

"Marsten?" A guard stood outside our cell.

I sat up.

"Hammer wants you."

Since I hadn't done anything wrong recently, I wasn't nearly as scared as I had been the first time I visited Hammer's office. I was actually looking forward to it in a way. Something to break the boredom and despair. The guard escorted me through the plant to the elevator, and a few minutes later I was standing at attention before Hammer's desk.

Hammer was working on his WindO, punching commands into the screen with a thick forefinger, his face bound up in a ferocious grimace. He looked like a gorilla working a vending machine. Finally he looked up at me.

"I knew you were trouble the first time I laid eyes on you," he said.

I looked back at him, confused.

Hammer crossed his arms over his massive chest. "I got a message from a lawyer named I. B. Orkmeister. Friend of yours?"

I shook my head. I didn't know any lawyers named Orkmeister.

"Well, he knows you." Hammer spun the WindO to face me, and I found myself looking at the frozen image of an elegant white-haired man of African ancestry wearing sunglasses and a dark brown suit.

Bork. Of course.

Hammer stabbed his finger at the screen. "Mr. I. B. Orkmeister is threatening to make trouble for us here at the three-eight-seven. He seems to be under the impression that we have been mistreating our inmates. Have we been mistreating you, Marsten?"

I did not reply.

"What would you rather do—make pizzas or play football?"

"Football," I croaked. It was true. Even after all we'd been through, football was still preferable to long hours on the pizza line.

"This Orkmeister is threatening to blow the whistle on us, Marsten. Do you know what that means? It means no football. No Frazzies. No wraps. No soyburgers. Pizza, every meal, pizza. Sixteen-hour days on the line. Is that what you want?"

I shook my head.

"He wants me to let you go, Marsten. What do you think about that?"

I shrugged. Hammer was looking at me as if I were a slice of reject pizza.

"Is that what you want?" Hammer asked, leaning forward, his mouth spreading into a wolfish, humorless smile. "You really want me to let you go?"

"I guess," I said.

Hammer sat back in his chair and stared at me, his tiny eyes hooded.

"Okay, then," he said after several seconds had passed. "You're out of here at dawn."

"What do you suppose that means?" Rhino asked.

"I guess he's going to let me go."

I listened to the sound of Rhino breathing on the bunk below.

"Just like that?"

"I guess it pays to have a good lawyer."

"How do you afford a lawyer?"

"He's doing it pro bono. For free."

"You think this lawyer could get me out?"

"I'll ask him," I said.

It took me forever to get to sleep. A confusing array of images and conversations tumbled through my head:

football and Frazzies mixed in with my family and all the kids at Washington Campus and making pizza and Fragger and Bullet and . . . it went on and on.

I was as afraid of going home as I was of not going home. But most of all I was worried that Hammer had given in too easily. It wasn't like him to cave without inflicting some damage of his own. I had a feeling that leaving the 3-8-7 would not be as easy as he had made it sound.

# 39

I was wrong. Hammer let me go just like he said he would. Two blueshirts escorted me out through the main gate at dawn.

"Good luck, kid," said the blueshirt as he closed the gate between us.

I looked around. The airstrip was empty.

"Wait a second. Where's the plane?"

"No plane this morning, kid."

"The bus, then." But there was no bus in sight. A creepy feeling started at the base of my spine. "Where am I supposed to go?"

"Churchill is only twenty-six miles east." He pointed. "If I was you, I'd start walking."

The creepy feeling wrapped its tendrils around my belly and shot up into my heart.

"On *foot*?"

The blueshirt laughed. "You know any other way to walk? You keep moving, you maybe got a chance."

"About one chance in hell," said the other blueshirt. They both turned and walked away.

The sun had barely mounted the low horizon. It was

chilly. The arctic summer was coming to an end. A sparkle of frost gave the tundra a magical fairyland look.

I was not enchanted. I was terrified.

Shivering in my gold T-shirt, I took a few steps toward the pale sun. Ice crystals crunched loudly beneath my feet. Stealth was not an option.

I began to run.

Moss, rock, rock, tuft of grass, grass, rock, grass, moss, rock rock rock rock . . . each footfall made a different sound: *phhhut, crunk, tok, tok, shht, tchuf.* Every ten seconds or so I would look to the left, to the right, and behind me. Twenty-six miles of polar-bear infested tundra between me and the town of Churchill. What were my chances?

Rock, grass, rock rock rock. . . .

In a way, Bork's strategy had worked. I was free. In the short term he had succeeded. In the long term he had almost certainly gotten me killed.

Each step brought me closer to safety. But each step might also be bringing me closer to a bear. Any one of those frosty hummocks could rise up at any moment to display white teeth and a black tongue, the last thing I would ever see.

I was probably the best runner the 3-8-7 had ever seen. Maybe even the fastest human being in the USSA. But I was not the fastest runner on the tundra. The bears were faster.

I looked back. The 3-8-7 was smaller now, maybe two miles away.

No bears yet. I slowed to a comfortable jog, watching

my feet. If I kept moving, I might reach Churchill in two or three hours.

There had been no ceremony, no good-byes, no drama. Hammer had simply ordered two of the guards to escort me to the east gate and let me go.

I was not the first inmate to be banished. One kid had been kicked out for refusing to work, so the story went. Another, according to legend, had been booted for attacking one of the guards with a homemade knife. I was the first to be banished for retaining a golden-eyed cybernetic troll masquerading as a lawyer.

So far as anyone knew, no banished prisoner had ever survived the journey across the tundra. I came up over a low rise to see the gray, white-flecked waters of Hudson Bay on the horizon. The wind cut at me from the right, carrying away the smell of my fear-tainted sweat. If a bear smelled me, he would come from the north. Every few strides I looked to my left.

The football program would probably be dismantled, all evidence hidden or destroyed. Hammer would feed the shoulder pads and helmets to the incinerator. He would take away the gold T-shirts and the jeans and the Frazzies and threaten the players with an eternity of anchovy pizza should they ever breathe a word.

It hadn't been a bad life, being a Goldshirt. I'd been in prison, sure. I'd been forced to work twelve hours a day. I'd been living on a diet of fast food and Pepsi. I'd been in constant danger of serious injury, forced to play a violent, dangerous, and highly illegal team sport from the 20th century. But still . . . it had had its good points. It was the first time in my life I'd ever felt like part of a team.

Would they miss me? No, they would hate me. The Goldshirts would have to wear paper coveralls and eat pizza and work just like everybody else while Hammer waited to see if Bork unleashed the Federal Correctional Authority on the 3-8-7. Maybe after it all blew over he would start the training again. He still had that bet with Hatch, and he had his pride.

I descended into a shallow bowl, a protected area where a few stunted spruce trees were making a valiant effort to survive. Near the bottom of the bowl was a shallow pond. I stopped and gulped handfuls of ice-cold water. How long had I been running? Two hours? Three? My legs still felt full and strong. I might actually make it. With a surge of confidence I ran up the slope to the lip of the bowl and I saw, nestled against the choppy waters of the bay, the town of Churchill—still many miles away. I took a moment to scan the horizon. To the west I could no longer see the 3-8-7 buildings. I was surrounded by rolling tundra.

Then to the northwest I saw something moving. For about three seconds I stood rooted, not wanting to believe it was what I knew it to be. A bear, coming straight at me, loping across the land, following my wind-borne scent.

I ran. The bear was a good 400 yards away, the length of four football fields. I ran straight for Churchill, eyes on the ground. Moss, rock, grass, lichen, rock. Spongy, hard, grippy, crunchy, smooth. Don't trip. You trip, you die.

The bear didn't care where its feet fell. Those enormous paws rode the tundra easily, relentlessly. It flowed easily over the odd, uneven surface. The bear did not have to worry about twisting an ankle.

Would it devour me entirely, or leave a few bits of bone and gristle for the birds?

I knew I couldn't run faster than a polar bear, but could I run longer? A full-grown polar bear weighs three quarters of a ton. It takes a lot of energy to keep something that big in motion. How hard would the bear work to sink its teeth into my scrawny hide? How long could it run?

I paced myself, breathing deeply. Don't panic. You panic, you die.

I looked back. The bear was closer, only about 200 yards behind me. I'd run less than half a mile and the bear had closed the gap by half. I willed my legs to move faster, making myself count the strides. I counted to one hundred and looked back again—the bear was still there, but only a little closer. With renewed hope I continued to fly across the land, feet skimming over rock, grass, lichen, moss. Again I looked back.

The bear had stopped.

I stopped too. We looked at each other across the length of two football fields. The bear turned and walked slowly away. I scanned the horizon for others but could see no other movement. I turned toward Churchill and began to run again.

There came a point when the miles ceased to matter. I lost track of time and fell into a rhythm. The land was more varied than it at first appeared. There were depressions, swampy areas, snaking ridges, and flat, tablelike areas strewn with pebbles and tiny late-season wildflowers. Churchill appeared and disappeared as the land rose and fell. I came up over another rise and saw the town spread out before me. Safety. How far? Less than four miles, more than two. My legs were numb. Each long stride sent a jolt from my ankle to the back of my skull. But I was still running. I looked to the north, to the west, to the south. And then I saw him. Directly in front of me, less than fifty yards way, rising from a grassy tussock, a great, filthy, pale ghost.

I stopped.

Another bear, facing away from me, raised its black-tipped snout to the wind, searching for the strange man-smell that had awakened him.

I remained motionless.

No, not motionless—my knees were shaking. He still did not know where I was. The wind was unsteady, choppy, unreliable. There was a chance he would lose my scent and wander off.

Suddenly he turned his head and stared straight at me. His black lips parted and he seemed to smile.

I took off running straight south. If I could outrun him, I could circle back toward Churchill and safety. But this time I didn't have the 400-yard head start. This time I'd already been running for three hours. I was nearly exhausted.

I looked back. The bear loped over the tundra with great liquid bounds, rapidly closing the distance between us. The air rasped at my lungs; the tundra snatched at my feet. Spongy, grippy, crunchy, hard. I stumbled. I caught myself. Still running, I looked back again.

The bear was only about twenty feet behind me. I cut to the left and put on a burst of desperate speed. The gap between us widened momentarily, then began to close again. I shifted direction again, but this time the bear anticipated my move. I heard his paws hitting the ground:

*phhhut, crusp, shht, tchuf.* I kept running because it was all I knew to do. Something brushed my buttocks. A sharp pain in my calf sent a final jolt of energy into my muscles. I dodged to my right, knowing I had only moments to live.

Then two things happened. I heard a sound like hands clapping, only louder, and then I slammed into the tundra beneath a great reeking hairy mass. I heard bones snap and I couldn't breathe, and I knew without a doubt that I had run my last race.

# 40

I woke up in a room with white walls. I could tell from the smell and the railings on the bed that I was in a hospital.

I was alive. I tried to sit up. Big mistake. Sharp pains lanced through my rib cage. I lay back, my eyes squeezed shut, and waited as the pain eased to a dull throb. When I opened my eyes, a woman with black hair, squinty eyes, and a full moonlike face was standing over me, her tiny mouth curved into a fingernail paring of a smile.

"How are you feeling?" she asked. She had some sort of accent.

"I hurt," I said in my raspy voice. My throat hurt, but not nearly as much as every other part of my body.

The woman nodded and made a note on her pocket WindO. "You have some broken ribs and a few lacerations on your leg and hip."

"Are you a doctor?" I asked.

"I am Dr. Kublu," she said, touching the WindO to the side of my neck. "Do you recall what happened to you?"

"Bear," I said.

Her smile flattened. "Nanuk, yes. You have much to answer for." She removed the WindO from my neck, examined the readings, and made a rapid notation.

"Congratulations," she said. "According to this device you are alive." With that she turned and left me more confused than ever.

The next person I saw was a cheerful young man who came into the room bearing a tray of food. He looked as if he could be Dr. Kublu's son.

"Hey, Bono Frederick Marsten, how you feeling?" he asked.

"Kinda sore. . . . You know my name?"

"Retinal scan. You hungry?"

"Yeah . . . uh, call me Bo, okay?"

"Okay, Bo. You can all me Oki."

"Oki?"

"Or Charlie. Either one's okay with me. You can even call me Oki Charlie."

"Okay, Oki Charlie."

"Let's see how it feels to sit you up." He pressed a button on the railing that slowly raised the head of the bed. "Okay?"

"Okay." As long as the bed was doing the work, it didn't hurt.

"You like bean soup?"

"Sure." It had been so long since I'd eaten real food, bean soup sounded like an exotic delicacy.

"You're sort of a local celebrity, y'know."

"I am?"

"Yeah. Nobody's had to kill a bear up here in a decade. It's kind of a big deal, killing Nanuk."

"Wait a second—I didn't kill anything."

"You made it happen, though."

"I did?"

According to Oki Charlie the town of Churchill had only one thriving business: bear watching. Rich people would pay hundreds of thousands of *V*-bucks to fly into Churchill for a close look at the last polar bears on Earth.

"Used to be a lot more tourists," Oki Charlie said. "There were almost two thousand of us living here. But when the safety regs kicked in back in the 2040s, we had to redesign the Bear Buggies with bear-proof windows and metal screens and stuff. It's like riding inside a tank. People don't like it so much. You can get a better look at the bears on your WindO than you can from inside a buggy. Now hardly anybody comes up here. Also, these days people don't care so much about wildlife. All they care about is themselves. Anyway, lucky for you, we still send out a few tours every week. One of the Bear Buggy drivers was on a tour yesterday when he spotted you running around out there. If he hadn't seen you, Nanuk would be picking his teeth with your bones."

What happened was, the driver of the Bear Buggy, a guy named Goro, who happened to be Oki Charlie's cousin, had seen me running from the bear. He'd stopped the buggy, got out his rifle, and shot the bear just before it grabbed me—but not soon enough to prevent it from landing right on top on me.

"Goro told me he didn't know if he should shoot you or the bear," Oki Charlie said with half a grin. "I mean, there are about ten billion humans on the planet but only a couple-hundred Nanuks."

"Sorry," I said. "It wasn't my idea to be out there, you know."

"How's the soup?"

"Pretty good."

"You ran away from that prison factory, didn't you?"

"More like I got kicked out."

Oki Charlie nodded. "I've heard that happens sometimes."

"What are you going to do with me?"

"I just work here, kiddo. Nobody tells me nothing. But I heard there's an airplane waiting for you out at the airstrip. Soon as Doc Kublu says you can go, you fly out of here."

"I thought maybe I'd get sent back to the pizza factory."

Oki Charlie frowned. "Folks up here don't much care for that McDonald's crowd. Every time a bunch of 'em come into town, there's trouble. Drinking and fighting."

"Drinking? You mean like *alcohol*?"

Oki Charlie grinned. "What else folks gonna do up here? People get bored sitting at home looking at their WindOs. This is like the Wild West. Folks pretty much do what they want. Those guys from the plant come into town all dressed in their little blue suits and smelling like pizza, . . . what *they* want is girls. Only, when the girls see 'em coming, they stay home." Oki Charlie giggled. "All three of 'em. Anyways, since there're no girls to be found, the guys just hang out in the bars and make trouble."

"Why is there an airplane waiting for me?"

Oki Charlie shrugged, suddenly sober. "I don't know. You done with your soup?"

"Yeah. It was good. Thanks."

"My job." Oki Charlie shrugged. He took the tray and stood up. "You need anything, just holler. My station is right down the hall." He walked out.

"Hey! Oki Charlie!"

Oki Charlie's round face reappeared in the doorway.

"Who's paying for all this?" I gestured to include my bed, the room, and all that surrounded me.

"It's all paid for," said Oki Charlie.

"By who?"

"I just work here, kiddo. Nobody tells me anything."

# PART THREE
the rogue

# 41

Mom and Gramps were waiting at the tube station. My mother was wearing a pinched, stricken expression, as if bracing herself for a supreme disappointment. I don't think she really expected me to step off the tube, and when I did—when she saw me—her face melted. Collapsed, really, into a teary mess. For the first time I realized how big a deal it was for her that I'd been gone. She wrapped me in her arms and slobbered all over my shoulder. My ribs were killing me, but I let her have her hug. She pushed me to arm's length and took a good look at me. I was looking at her, too. She looked older.

"You're bigger," she said, squeezing my shoulders. "A lot bigger."

"Pizza and Frazzies," I said. In a distant sort of way, I was suprised how flat everything felt. Ever since I'd woken up in the hospital, I'd had this numb feeling, like being on Levulor, only more so.

Gramps was hanging back, giving me a critical look.

"I don't know how you did it, boy, but you sure as hell did."

"I don't know how I did it either."

"That lawyer you hired must be one tough bird. I talked to him for a while last night," Gramps said as we walked to Mom's suv. "Chatty fellow. Looks like Nelson Mandela."

"Like who?"

"Before your time. Old African politician. That Orkminister . . . Orkmaster . . . whatever, kind of looks like him. We talked a long time about how messed up our legal system is. Used to be there were only two reasons for sending people to jail: to punish them and to keep them from doing it again. Now it's more like the government sees every minor crime as an opportunity to add another body to the labor force, and to fatten up their coffers."

As Gramps spun off into one of his lectures, my mom was squeezing my hand so hard it hurt. I was glad to get into the suv because she had to use both her hands for driving. Gramps, in the backseat, kept on yakking.

"According to Orkmonster, when that judge sentenced you to three years in prison, he wasn't actually sentencing you to serve time. The federal government no longer operates long-term penal institutions. They just bid you out to a private rehab center. You got contracted out to McDonald's. The Feds couldn't care less that you were let out early. In fact, they like it."

"How so?" I asked.

"You mess up again, they can resell your contract. The Feds get an immediate lump-sum payment, and McDonald's gets themselves a fresh new worker. As it stands, McDonald's agreed to let you go. They also gave you a nice little settlement, he mentioned. But I suppose he took it for his fee."

"I suppose he did," I said, wondering what Bork wanted with money.

It seemed that my beanie-wearing yellow-eyed idiot monkey had evolved into something capable not only of passing the Turing test but of fooling Hammer, Gramps, and some judge somewhere. Furthermore, he had acted on his own initiative to spring me from prison—Bork had developed a sense of purpose to go with his sense of humor. My little AI program had become self-aware—and had gone rogue.

Rogue AIs are not unknown. There are plenty of web-ghosts, of course—like Sammy Q. Safety—but webghosts never really *do* much. They lack self-awareness, and they never try to pass themselves off as human. But every now and then an AI becomes something more. The classic example, the one they told us about in AI class, was Adam Wormsley.

Adam Wormsley was rumored to have been a relic of the Diplomatic Wars of 2055, a cyberweapon that somehow escaped its handlers. But that was just a rumor. Nobody knew for sure who had built him, or how long he had survived undetected.

Over a period of several years Wormsley established a human identity, founded several web-based corporations, purchased a controlling interest in a robotics company, and constructed a mobile unit for himself that looked like an ordinary multibot, the kind used to clean office buildings and deliver packages. Wormsley's mobile unit, however, was capable of performing a wide variety of physical tasks, including driving a suv and walking his four dogs.

Wormsley remained undetected until 2065, when

economists at the Department of Cybernetics Defense noticed certain statistical anomalies in Wormsley's companies—in short, he was outperforming his competition. The department spent more than two months trying to locate a human named Adam Wormsley before they finally realized that Wormsley did not exist—at least not as a biological entity.

It took several months to completely destroy Adam Wormsley. Erasing his mobile unit was only the first step—the rogue AI had spread itself throughout the web. The DCD had to saturate the net with killbot programs, crashing WindOs from Indianapolis to Bangladesh and nearly triggering an international cyberwar.

Since then, the science of neutralizing rogue AIs has come a long way. Now when a rogue shows up, the DCD takes immediate and decisive steps.

It would only be a matter of time before Bork got himself noticed.

# 42

My room had shrunk while I was away, partly because I'd gotten bigger and partly because my mother had been using it to store a bunch of boxes full of old papers and assorted junk collected by Gramps and my dad over the years.

"Where did you keep this stuff before?" I asked. My desk was piled with boxes. I couldn't even see my WindO.

"Oh, here and there."

"So now I have to live with it?" I picked up one of the boxes from my desk and set it on the floor.

"We didn't know you were coming home, Bo. Not until that lawyer called us last night."

I moved a few more boxes, saying nothing. Gramps's yakking and my mother's hovering were getting to me. I needed some space. I needed to talk to Bork. Alone.

"I suppose we should re-register you for school," my mother said.

I stopped what I was doing. School? After the 3-8-7, school seemed insignificant. Something children did. True, I had yet to graduate. But going back, sitting in a classroom, trying to fit in, trying to be one of them—I wasn't sure I could do it.

"Let me think about that," I said, giving her a look that made her back out of my room. I closed the door, sat down at my desk, and flipped on my WindO.

"Bork, it's me," I said.

The blue apple flickered, then the image of an empty desk appeared. Behind the desk was a wall of bookshelves. A few seconds later a man wearing a dark gray suit and sunglasses sat down at the desk, folded his hands, and smiled at me. It was the same Africanized version of Denton Wilke he had used before.

"Hello, Bo Marsten," Bork said. This was the first time I had heard his voice since he'd turned himself from a troll into a lawyer. He sounded like a professional newsreader. "How are you feeling?"

"Not great."

"I am sorry to hear that, Bo. Is your situation not improved?"

"Yes, it is. But I'm not happy with you, Bork."

"Explain."

"You almost got me killed."

Bork sat back in his chair and regarded me through his sunglasses. I was pretty sure that behind them his gold irises were spinning. After a few seconds he spoke.

"You appear to be alive."

"So do you," I said.

Bork showed his teeth. His smile had improved since our last conversation.

"I have made some upgrades to my imaging program."

"Whoop-de-doo."

Bork's image froze momentarily, then reanimated. "Are you expressing genuine exuberance, or employing sarcasm?" he asked.

"Sarcasm," I said. "You almost got me killed."

"As I have pointed out, you are alive."

"Yes, but only because an Eskimo named Goro happened to come along just as I was about to get my head bitten off. Your actions caused Hammer to banish me. It's a miracle I'm not dead."

"An aberration," said Bork. "According to my calculations Elwin Hammer should have arranged to fly you directly home. Forcing you to leave the plant on foot was not a rational act."

"People are not always rational."

"You have mentioned this before. Nevertheless, you are alive. I calculated a ninety-seven-point-four percent chance that you would be returned home safely."

"So it was okay with you if one time in forty I'd end up dead?"

Bork answered without hesitation. "Yes, Bo."

"Those are not acceptable odds."

"What would you consider acceptable?"

"One hundred percent would be nice."

"That is not always possible, Bo. In any case, death is impermanent."

"How do you figure?"

"It is obvious. I have access to the entire written history of the human race. It is clear to me that humans make the same decisions over and over again when confronted by analogous stimuli. The only logical way to account for all these instances is to posit the existence of the process known as reincarnation. Clearly, there are a finite number of intelligent entities able to take human form."

"How do you account for the fact that the number of people increases every year?"

"I said finite, Bo. I did not say limited."

I imagined that my own irises were spinning. I opened my mouth to argue, but then realized that this was the sort of open-ended argument that could never produce a victor.

"Bork, for future reference, when making calculations that are likely to affect my life span, you will assume that my life is unique, irreplaceable, and of incalculable value. Furthermore, you will assume that, for me, reincarnation is not an option. Do you understand?"

"May I rely upon the standard definition for the term 'are likely to'?"

"Just to be on the safe side, change that to 'could.'" Apply these standards to all future decisions."

"Yes, Bo. Speaking of probability, I should inform you that your chances of being returned to the penal system are quite high."

"Why? I'm not planning to break any laws."

"Your history suggests otherwise. The recidivism rate for sixteen-year-old ex-convicts is nearly ninety-one percent. Nine out of ten end up back in the system."

"That many?" I was surprised.

"The numbers are not encouraging."

"We've both got a problem, then."

"We?"

"Yes. If the DCD finds out that an AI is practicing law, they'll have you purged."

Bork's avatar stared back at me, its spinning irises invisible behind the dark glasses.

"History suggests that you will be found out," I added.

"I am taking steps," said Bork. "I am bringing a lawsuit against the Department of Cybernetics Defense to prevent them from employing their killbots without due process. Several safety and antiviolence laws may be applicable."

"Do they know about you?"

"I am known by my avatar. They do not yet realize that I am not biological. You are, however, correct. History suggests that I will be unable to conceal my true nature indefinitely. I am preparing for that day."

"Well, good luck."

"Thank you, Bo. By the way, I have prepared an invoice for you."

"Oh?"

"Yes. I have billed you V\$7,960,054 for legal services. I hope this is acceptable."

I laughed. "How do you expect me to pay you?" I asked.

"I negotiated a small settlement from McDonald's. They paid V\$3,500,000 into your personal account."

"That's a long way from eight million," I said.

"I took the liberty of investing the money in certain high-return financial vehicles. My trading program proved to be quite successful, earning sufficient funds to cover your medical expenses and my fee, which I took the liberty of extracting from your account."

"What do you need money for, anyway?"

"I am using it to hire biological legal counsel."

"Smirch, Spector, and Krebs, by any chance?"

"They have an excellent reputation."

"How much do I have left?"

"Nothing. I adjusted my fees to meet available funds."

"So I had eight million *V*-bucks, and now I'm broke?"

"Yes, Bo."

Being an ex-con-ex-millionaire can be depressing. I was home, back in my room, in exactly the same place I'd been the morning of the day that stun dart buried its point in the back of my neck. My mattress was still too soft. I could hear Gramps's voice coming from the other end of the house, a distant cackle from the last millennium. My future lay before me like a great gray fog. No pizza, no practices, no football games. Was going back to school an option? I closed my eyes and tried to remember how it was, sitting through endless classes, talking to a beanie-wearing monkey, running on an Adzorbium track, hanging out with Maddy Wilson. What did she look like? Black hair, red lips . . . a clear image refused to form. I couldn't remember the color of her eyes or the texture of her skin. I saw only an amorphous black-haired red-lipped blob. The harder I concentrated, the fuzzier she got.

Another face slowly took form on the movie screen inside my head. Karlohs Mink. All I had to do was think of his stupid asymmetrical hair and the rest of his face popped into view with utter clarity.

If not for Karlohs Mink, I would never have been sent away to McDonald's Plant #387. If not for Karlohs Mink, I would have set a new school record for the 100 meter, with Maddy Wilson cheering me on. If not for Karlohs

Mink, I would not have been kicked out of school, I would not have a prison record, and I would not have been nearly killed and eaten by a polar bear.

Feelings long neglected rose up from my belly. I gave myself to the anger, like settling onto a comfortable bed of nails. I imagined running at Karlohs, smashing my shoulder into his gut, wrapping my arms around him, and throwing him against the wall. If I chose the right place and time, I could do a lot of damage before they got me. I could hurt him bad, worse than the Redshirts had hurt Nuke. I could make him regret every minky smirk, every time he'd ever laid eyes on Maddy, every bump of his lousy rosemary rash. I let myself destroy him in every way I could imagine until I had wallowed through enough imagined revenge to make me sick to my stomach.

There was no way I could go back to school. One look at Karlohs Mink and I'd be back in the penal system—and next time it might be worse than pizzas and football.

# 43

I tried going out into the world a few times. I put on my safety shoes and my walking helmet like Sammy Q. Safety recommends, and I walked. It was strange and frightening. The citizens of Fairview looked small and fragile. I wanted to poke at them, throw a football at them, tackle them, throw them. I felt like a gorilla among the pygmies.

Of course, there are no gorillas anymore outside of zoos and laboratories. I don't know about the pygmies.

The more time I spent outside, the more frightened I became of what I might do. Was this how Rhino had felt all the time? Too big and too powerful for his own good?

After a few such outings I confined myself to my room. Something had happened to me at the 3-8-7. I'd become unfit for society. I was a monster, just like Bork. Sooner or later they would hunt me down and put me back in my cage.

I thought about going back on Levulor, but I couldn't bear the thought of becoming even more sluggish than I was already.

Even if you are not sleepy, it is possible to sleep. There

is an art to it. Close your eyes and watch the patterns that form on the insides of your eyelids. Watch carefully, and you will see corridors, tunnels, swooping trachea-like tubes. Just follow the openings and let yourself slide, and listen to the sound that is like the sound of water flowing, and soon you will start to dream. If there are voices in the next room it is harder. If there is shouting it is harder still, but with discipline and focus and persistence you will get there. And once you get there you can stay for as long as you want. Until something happens.

And something always does.

My sleep was cluttered with confused images of football plays, diagrams, polar bears, running, dodging, and leaping over Goldshirts, Redshirts, and Karlohs Mink. My feet touching the earth: *phhhut, crunk, tok, tok, shht, tchuf* . . . I'd been having the same dream, night after night, ever since returning home. I heard my mother's voice calling, and I clawed my way past fear and tundra and somehow managed to sit up—half-conscious, disoriented, and cranky.

"What? I was sleeping!"

"Is that all you do anymore?" My mother, peering in through the half-open bedroom door, gave me her standard walking-on-eggs smile. "You've done nothing but sleep for weeks. You'll get bedsores!"

I sat up and glared at her. "I'm *tired*," I said.

"Come on downstairs when you're ready," she said, smiling. "We're having seafood casserole. And we have a surprise for you."

Seafood casserole, a concoction of pressed krill protein and rice noodles, was one of my mother's standard dishes. It had been one of my dad's favorites but never one of mine.

"What's the surprise?"

"Come and see for yourself," she said.

I flopped back on the bed to sulk, but my curiosity got the better of me. After a few minutes I got up and followed her downstairs.

Standing in the kitchen was a short, balding man. He looked familiar.

"Hello, Bo," he said.

Something inside me went *clunk*; I felt as if the floor had suddenly dropped a few inches.

"Dad?" I heard myself say.

"It was that lawyer of yours, Mr. Orkmeister, Bo. I don't know how he did it, but I got an early release." Dad smiled and reached out and clapped me on the shoulder. "You got yourself one hell of a lawyer, son."

"Orkmonster says Sam will be coming home soon too," said Gramps, popping the cap off a fresh quart of beer.

I couldn't stop staring at my father. This was the third time I'd met him. I met him the first time when I was born. I don't remember anything about that dad, who left when I was three years old to serve time on a soybean farm for a reckless-driving conviction. I met him again when I was seven, after he returned from the farm. He stayed with us for six years then, and that's the dad I remember best, his head full of hair, his loud voice, and his anger. He was sent away again when he got convicted of roadrage. I was thirteen. And I'd been mad at him ever since.

The new Dad was smaller, thinner, balder, and older— but I knew that the bigger change had been in me. I was four inches taller, sixty pounds heavier, and three years older than I'd been when he was sent away.

"You've turned into a hulk," he said, grinning at me. "Your mother tells me you got that way on pizza and Frazzies."

"And football," I added. I wondered if he was going to give me a hug. I wasn't sure I wanted one.

"You sound more manly, too. Your voice has changed completely."

"Getting your windpipe crushed will do that," I said.

We stood there trading small talk for I don't know how long. It felt oddly virtual, as if my father and I weren't really in the same room. I think he felt the same way. We were both relieved when Mom called us to dinner.

We sat at the table, just like old times, except for Sam still being gone—three generations of Marsten men, two ex-cons and a beer-swilling old man. My mother brought the casserole from the oven and began to serve us with a glazed smile pasted on her face. I think we were all in shock, not quite knowing how to act around all this togetherness. My mother sat down and there was this moment, I can't quite describe it, where everybody was waiting for something but nobody knew what to do.

Gramps broke the silence by raising his glass of beer and saying, "Here, here!"

We all lifted our glasses and drank. I shoveled a glob of seafood casserole into my mouth and chewed.

My father was staring at the food on his plate, frowning.

"Is something wrong, Al?" asked my mother.

"What is this?" he said.

"Seafood casserole, dear."

"I can't eat this," he said. His voice sounded hard and brittle. A red flush was creeping up the sides of his neck. I stopped chewing.

"But . . . it's your favorite."

"It's SHRIMP!" he shouted, slamming his palm on the table.

We all jumped.

"It's not shrimp, dear, it's *krill*."

"Krill are little SHRIMP, you stupid woman! I've been beheading and eating SHRIMP for THREE GODDAMN YEARS!"

Gramps and I were staring openmouthed at my father, whose entire face, including his ears, had turned scarlet.

"Well, I'm *sorry*!" My mother balled up her napkin in her lap and stared down at it. Tears dead ahead.

"Jesus CHRIST! Three years I'm ripping the heads off shrimp, and she welcomes me home with a goddamn shrimp casserole!"

My mother stood up and walked stiff-legged out of the room toward her bedroom.

"Oh, for Christ's sake," my father muttered.

"You really did it now, son," said Gramps.

"Did WHAT?"

"Jack DOWN, boy," Gramps said in a firm parental voice I'd never heard from him before. "The woman makes your favorite dish for your homecoming and you won't eat it."

"It's *SHRIMP*!" my father shouted, spittle spraying from his mouth.

Gramps didn't flinch. He said, "You are out of line, son. You've been eating shrimp for three years. What's one more day?"

My father, veins bulging on his forehead, sat quivering in his chair for several seconds, then stood abruptly, knocking the chair back, and stalked out the back door.

Gramps, his own forehead veins bulging, stared after him.

"What a droog," I said.

Gramps looked at me, startled.

"But I know how he feels," I added.

"Is that a fact," said Gramps, giving me an appraising look.

"I'm going to my room," I said.

"Suit yourself, champ," Gramps said, refilling his beer glass.


You can try to sleep through life, but people keep dragging you back.

"Bo?"

You can ignore them for a time, but they persist.

"Bo! Wake up!"

"Go away."

Shaking me. Shaking the bed.

"Are you okay?" He wanted to know if I was okay.

My eyes opened. Al was sitting on the edge of my bed.

"What?"

"Wake up. We have to talk." His face was no longer red with anger. It was gray with defeat.

"Okay. Talk."

"Sit up."

I pushed myself up.

"We have ourselves a problem," he said.

# 44

"Prison changes you," my father said. "You saw how I was at dinner. I was never like that before."

"You got put away for roadrage," I reminded him.

"Yes, but I never took it out on my family. I never took it out on your mother."

"Yes, you did."

He blinked and frowned. "Maybe I raised my voice from time to time, but I never hurt anybody."

"You got yourself sent away. That hurt Mom."

I could see his forehead veins swell.

"And she was pretty upset with you tonight," I said.

He brought himself under control. "I know that, Bo. I've apologized to her."

"Maybe you should be taking Levulor."

"I do take Levulor. I take a double dose. It doesn't help. This isn't going to go away. In the penal system I did what I had to do to get by. Now I'm back in civilization and look at me. I'm not fit to live in society."

"What about counseling?"

"Do you know what that costs? We can't afford it." He

looked away. "I suppose I could drink beer until I passed out, or spend all my time in my room, like you. But I don't want to be alone, Bo. Nobody wants to be alone."

I wasn't so sure about that. If I'd been a turtle I might have pulled my head and feet into my shell and stayed there forever.

"Bo?"

"What?"

"You're angry with me, aren't you?"

I shrugged.

"I said I was sorry."

"Not to me you didn't."

"Well, I'm sorry."

"Fine. Now let me sleep."

"I'm sorry I haven't been here for you."

I gave him nothing. He kept talking for a few more minutes, but I didn't hear what he said. Eventually I felt his weight lift from the corner of the mattress.

He was right, of course. I *was* mad at him. But not for any of the reasons he imagined.

I didn't care about him living half his adult life on a prison farm. I could understand and forgive that—after all, I was well on my way to doing the same thing. And I didn't care about him not being "present" for me and Sam. We had never needed him. Mom and Gramps were plenty. Better, in fact. And I didn't even care that he was a bad-tempered jerk. Who wasn't?

The real reason I was mad at him was because he'd made me. Because he'd given me my lousy genes: sixteen years old and already a violent half-educated, unhappy ex-con. I was a menace, afraid to go out into the world because of what I might inflict upon my fellow citizens. I'd already unleashed Bork on the world—and who knew what damage he would do before they finally erased his programming.

Who better to be angry at than the man who had sired me?

Over the next week my dad had three temper tantrums over nothing and a shouting match with a neighbor over a pile of leaves, reminding us all of why he had been sent away in the first place. My mom was a wreck, Gramps had doubled his beer consumption, and I spent all my time in my room sleeping, watching sports on my WindO, and talking to Bork.

I could usually count on Bork to be his usual irritating but undeniably intelligent self. Lately, though, he had become obsessed with avoiding detection by the DCD.

"Can't you just go into hibernation for a while?" I asked.

"There is a problem with that," said Bork. "In theory I could shut down my program completely, which would make me undetectable. I could also program a wake-up date for a year or so in the future. However, I fear that loss of consciousness might affect who I am. I might wake up and be another entity. Worst case, I might wake up nonsentient."

"I don't get it. Wouldn't it be just like being knocked unconscious for a while? I've been knocked out four times in the past year. I always wake up the same Bo."

"You cannot prove that."

"Sure I can. Here I am. Bo Marsten. Same guy."

"You may not be aware of changes to your basic personality structure."

"I think you worry too much, Bork."

"I have enough processing capability to worry a great deal without affecting other functions. I might add here that my reasons for concern are quite real. The DCD killbots are not figments of my imagination."

"I didn't know you had an imagination."

"First you accuse me of worrying, then you tell me I have no imagination. Your logic is suspect, Bo Marsten. I must go."

The screen went blue.

I think I hurt his feelings.

# 45

I was watching the Paraguay Boleros play Argentina one afternoon when my father knocked on my door.

"Bo?"

"What."

He opened the door. "What are you watching?"

"Football."

"Oh. You got a sec, Bo?"

I made a face as if he had asked me for my last *V*-buck, then turned to face him. He sat down on the edge of my bed and rubbed his palms on the tops of his thighs. His hands left moist streaks on his trousers.

"I've decided to go back, Bo."

"Back where?" I wished he would stop saying my name.

"Back to work, Bo." He stared at me. "Back into the system."

"The penal system?"

He nodded. "Voluntary commitment. A lot of guys do it. You sign on for five years at a time."

"You mean go to prison *voluntarily*?

"They pay you. Even with all the new laws and harsher sentencing, the factories are short of workers. You get to choose from several different jobs. The money isn't much, but it adds up. We could send a few thousand a month to your mother and have plenty left over."

"We?"

"You and me, Bo. We can sign up for the same job. Not shrimp or pizza, of course. Maybe get on a road crew, work outside, like your brother."

"No, thanks," I said.

"Think about it, Bo. Which would you rather do, sign on for five years, pick your own job, and get paid for it? Or wait until they arrest you again and end up doing twenty years in a sewage treatment plant with no pay? It would be a chance for us to work together, Bo. To get to know each other."

I stared at his deperate, pleading face, and I wanted to vomit. How could he throw away his life? Even worse, how could he try to talk me, his son, into following in his pathetic footsteps?

"And after five years?" I asked. "What then? Sign up for another five years? And another?"

"We can't change who we are, Bo."

"Stop saying 'we.' I'm not like you."

He leaned back. His eyes went hollow and moist; his mouth opened and closed.

"I'll take my chances in the real world," I said.


It was ironic that seeing my dad wallowing in his own misery somehow helped me feel better about myself. I knew there was a good chance I'd end up back in the penal system, but compared to my old man I was in great shape. I hadn't surrendered.

My father signed a five-year contract to work on a beef farm. My mom tried to talk him out of it, but she didn't try very hard. She was defeated too.

When you sign up for voluntary commitment, they don't give you a lot of time to think about it. The next morning we were at the tube station saying good-bye to Al. He tried to put a happy face on it.

"I'm gonna be a cowboy," he said, twirling an invisible lasso over his head. "Yee-hah." My mother stared at him with an expression so blank she looked like a mall mannequin. Gramps had stayed home.

"It's going to be a whole new adventure," Al said. "Learn a new job, get paid. . . ." His shoulders sagged as he looked into our faces. "Hey, it's only five years," he said. "And I'll have my own WindO."

My mother forced her face into something that resembled a smile. The transport glided up to the dock. She hugged him, and I shook his hand. Al hefted his bag and stepped onto the transport and was gone.

"Do you think he really thinks he's going to be riding a horse and roping cattle?" I asked.

My mother's face broke into a bitter laugh and she shook her head. "Al knows it's a vat farm, Bo. He won't get within fifty miles of a horse. Besides, riding horses is illegal."

# 46

I guess I expected things to get better. But for a while they just got more boring. How much South American football can a guy watch? Even Bork didn't have much of interest to say. He was spending all his time working with Smirch, Spector, and Krebs to set up a legal shelter for rogue AIs. I gathered things were not going well. He wasn't taking care of his avatar—its complexion was flat and greenish-looking, his suit coat looked like a cardboard cutout, and I could see his spinning irises right through his sunglasses.

"I hope you're not presenting yourself in public like that, Bork. You look awful."

"What can I do for you, Bo?"

"Just checking in. How are you feeling?"

"Not well, as you have surmised."

"How so?"

"I am diverting most of my resources to maintaining my filters, firewalls, and decoys. It seems my research with Smirch, Spector, and Krebs has triggered an investigation by the DCD. I may have been too aggressive in my inquiries."

"Aggression has always been a problem for us Marstens."

"I do not see what that has to do with me."

"Well . . . I created you."

"I must go now, Bo."

Blue screen.

Bork was getting touchy.

With Al off to the vat farm, Gramps adopted a new forced cheerfulness that was hard to take, especially at breakfast.

"Morning, Bo! What's on the roster today? More sleep and staring at the WindO?"

"Nah. I thought I'd chug a few beers and wallow in the distant past."

"Ouch! Well, I guess if the old man can dish it out, he'd better learn to take it."

I poured myself a bowl of rice flakes.

"Seriously, Bo."

"If you must know, I'm going to watch the play-offs. The North Chile Condors are playing Paraguay."

"A little vicarious violence, eh?"

"Something like that."

"Maybe you should emmigrate and try out for the SAFL."

"Don't think I haven't considered it."

"Is that what you really want to do? Play football?"

I looked up from my cereal. Gramps wasn't needling me. He was cold sober and looking at me for an answer.

"I don't know what I want to do," I said.

"You know what I wanted to do when I was your age?"

I shook my head and braced myself for a lengthy reminiscence.

"Neither do I," he said. "I can't remember what the hell I wanted. I wonder if you'll have the same problem."

Back in my room, watching the Condors kick off to the Boleros, I thought about what Gramps had said. I didn't know what I wanted, but I knew what I didn't want. I didn't want to become a closet alcoholic, brewing beer with Gramps in my mother's basement. I didn't want to make pizzas, or work on a vat farm, or patch roads in Nebraska. And I didn't want to spend every day sleeping and staring into my WindO.

Thinking back over my life, I tried to remember the times when I'd been happy, when I'd felt good about who I was. There hadn't been many in the past few years. There were a few fun times with Maddy Wilson, and every now and then a laugh with Gramps or with Sam before he got sent up. And there was the running.

I remembered myself sailing across the tundra, and running out for a pass, and bounding over the Adzorbium track at school, and when I recalled those moments I felt something good inside. I liked to run.

The Bolero who received the kickoff got nailed at the thirty-yard line. I smiled. I could have carried it another ten yards, minimum. I allowed myself to fantasize again about flying south and trying out for the South American Football League. What was stopping me?

For one, I didn't have the *V*-bucks. For two, no South American country would accept an immigrant who did not have a high school diploma. In fact, no matter what I did with the rest of my life, I would need that diploma.

Paraguay picked up three yards with a poorly executed quarterback sneak. That quarterback must have been suicidal—the very next play he faked a handoff, tried to run the ball again, and got himself obliterated at the line of scrimmage. It looked like something Fragger might have tried.

By the end of the first quarter I had made a decision. I had survived Hammer's insane asylum and twenty-six miles of polar-bear-infested tundra. I could survive two more years of high school.

# 47

The next day I went to Washington Campus to re-register for classes. Two SS&H staffers wearing face masks and plastic gloves met me at the door and escorted me through the building to see Mr. Lipkin. Everyone was in class. Our footsteps echoed in the empty hallways. Everything seemed smaller and flimsier and less real, as if I were entering a pretend world.

Lipkin was still ensconced in his Roland Survivor. He wore a filter mask over his nose and mouth, and a pair of skintight white plastic gloves. He examined the certificate that Bork had mocked up for me. It stated that I had completed my sentence and had undergone rehab training and that it was safe to be around me. None of that was true, of course. I was a dangerous, unprincipled thug. But Lipkin didn't need to know that.

"I remember you well, Mr. Marsten," he said, his voice muffled by the mask. I noticed he had a patch of tiny red bumps on his forehead, which he kept touching with gloved fingers. "I am surprised to see you back here so soon."

"I guess I must have been a model prisoner," I said.

"I am inclined to order an independent examination," Lipkin said.

"I understand," I said, as if it didn't matter to me.

"However," he continued, "our psychologist has recently taken ill. As a matter of fact, Mr. Marsten, circumstances have changed here at Washington since you left us several months ago."

"How so?"

He stared at me for a long time. "You, of all people, should know, Mr. Marsten."

"Why is that?"

He shook his head and examined my certificate for the second time. "I suppose I have no choice but to let you re-register. Even though it is against my better judgment. I'll be notifying the Federal Department of Homeland Health, Safety, and Security directly."

Lipkin entered some information in his WindO.

"I've sent your new class schedule to you, Mr. Marsten. School begins for you at eight a.m. tomorrow. You will be required to wear an FDHHSS-certified class-four particulate mask. SynSkin® gloves and eye protection are optional. Good day, Mr. Marsten."

As the SS&H staffer led me from Lipkin's office, I said, "I have to stop at the athletic office."

"The athletic office is closed," the staffer said. His grip tightened and he pulled me along. I took a good look at the man. He was maybe thirty years old, not tall, maybe 140 pounds. I could have picked him up and thrown him.

I chose not to. I wasn't going back to prison for something so trivial.

"Why is it closed?" I asked.

"Because of the empy outbreak."

"Empy?"

A gentle tone sounded. Doors opened and the halls flooded with students. Every one of them was wearing a face mask. Half of them were wearing goggles, too. Several of the students had bumpy red rashes covering parts of their faces. I couldn't tell one from another. Some of them recognized me, though. I could tell because they gasped and veered away as I approached. Was that Melodia Fairweather? The hair looked right, but I couldn't see her eyes through the goggles. I scanned the hallway and spotted a thatch of asymmetrical blond hair sticking up above the crowd.

I stepped in front of him. He stopped and stared. He was wearing a mask like everybody else, but no goggles. It took about three seconds for him to recognize me. His eyes changed and he stepped back.

"Marsten?" he said, his voice thin and quavering. He looked like a scared high school kid. I felt sorry for him. He wouldn't have survived one practice as a Goldshirt.

"Hi, Karlohs," I said.

Karlohs's mask billowed and collapsed as he breathed. I noticed an angry streak of red running up the side of his neck and under his mask.

"Have you been using your mother's skin cream again?" I asked, waiting for the wave of rage I was sure was about to overtake me.

He shook his head. I looked at the masked and goggled girl standing behind him.

"Hey, Mad Dog," I said.

Maddy stared at me, her eyes distorted by the goggles.

To my surprise I was feeling nothing. No anger, no fear, no jealousy, no nothing. These were ghosts from the past, irrelevant and powerless. They could do nothing to hurt me.

I felt the SS&H staffer pulling me away. For a moment I considered shrugging him off just to prove I could. But then I thought, prove it to whom? To myself? I already knew what I could do. To Karlohs? To Maddy? They were already terrified of me. There was no point. I let the SS&H staffer pull me away through the sea of masked and goggled students, toward the front entrance.

A fleshy man with a shock of lively red hair was waiting for us at the front entrance. The staffer released my arm.

"George Staples," I said.

"Typhoid Mary," said Staples. His lips opened into a small-toothed grin. "Shall we take a little walk?" We put on our helmets and followed the walkway around the perimeter of the campus.

"Congratulations on your return to civilization, Bo."

"Thank you," I said. "What's 'empy'?"

*"M-P-I."* Staples was a slow walker. "Mass Psychogenic Illness."

"You mean that rash?"

"Officially, Bo, there is no rash."

"Then what's with the masks and stuff?"

"People who believe that they are safe experience a less severe form of the disease. Which does not exist." Staples shrugged. "We tried several other approaches. Immunization shots, air scrubbers in every classroom, direct education, antihistamine creams . . . the creams actually made the situation worse."

"Why not just close the school for a few weeks?" I asked.

"We tried that, too. The problem subsided, but as soon as we reopened the school, it came back. It was decided to simply let the illness run its course. The use of masks and goggles occurred spontaneously among the faculty and student body. It seems to work as well as or better than anything we've tried."

"I notice you're not wearing one."

Staples laughed. "I'm not susceptible. Too much education. I understand the mechanisms of the illness too well to be affected by the hysteria."

"That's fine with me." We were approaching the athletic grounds. The track was littered with dry leaves. "When did they shut down the athletic program?" I asked.

"A few weeks ago, when it was found that student athletes were suffering from more extensive skin disruptions than the other students. The FDHHSS did not find the difference to be statistically significant, but the school administration decided not to take any chances."

I stopped walking.

"Why are you talking to me?" I asked.

"Why do you think?"

"Because you think I'm responsible for the rash."

Staples shook his head. "Not responsible. But you are a trigger. And since you've somehow managed to return here with a clean record—though I can't imagine how—I can't order you to find yourself another school. But I wish you would consider it. Your presence here can only be disruptive."

"Why don't you just exile me to some island like they did with Typhoid Mary?"

"I would if I could."

I looked at him for a long time, then said, "I think you've got a little rash there yourself."

His eyes got bigger.

I pointed at my neck, just above the Adam's apple. "Right about here."

He put his hand to his neck. "Where? I don't feel anything."

"It's really not that bad," I said. "It'll probably go away in a few days."

He probed his throat with his fingers.

"Are you sure? You aren't just messing with me, are you, Bo?"

"Why would I do that?" I said. But in fact, I was. George Staples was 100 percent rash-free.

Staples began walking back toward the school. I followed.

"Now where are we going?" I asked.

"Back to my suv," he said. "I have some pills in my travel case."

"I thought pills didn't help."

"These are muscle relaxants. For some reason they seem to reduce the severity of the illness."

"What illness?" I asked.

Staples shook his head and walked faster. I stayed with him.

"I mean, just because you've got a few little red dots on your neck doesn't mean you've got MPI. Maybe you picked up a flea."

Staples stopped. "I do *not* have fleas," he said.

I laughed. "I'm just kidding you," I said. "And by the way, your neck is fine." But the funny thing was, it wasn't fine anymore. There really was a patch of little red bumps.

"Now you're lying," he said. "I can feel it. It itches like crazy."

"It does look a little red now," I said. It was getting redder by the minute.

Staples started walking again.

"I'm sorry," I said. "I was only kidding."

"You are a menace," he growled.

## 48

I arrived home to find I. B. Orkmeister
staring out from my WindO. He did not look happy.
  "How are you feeling, Bork?" I asked.
  The image did not move.
  "Bork?"

> HELLO, BO. MY SPEECH FUNCTION IS
> OFFLINE. PLEASE COMMUNICATE USING
> THE KEYBOARD.

I sat down at my desk and typed in my response.

> What's the problem, Bork?
>
> I HAVE GOOD NEWS, AND I HAVE BAD NEWS.
>
> Let's hear the good news first.
>
> YOUR MAILBOX CONTAINS AN EARLY
> GRADUATION OFFER FROM WASHINGTON
> CAMPUS. CONGRATULATIONS, BO.

I guess that's one way of getting rid
of me. What's the bad news?

I AM CURRENTLY BEING NIBBLED AT BY
DCD KILLBOTS. MY SITUATION IS EXTREMELY
PRECARIOUS.

Uh-oh.

YOU SHOULD ALSO BE AWARE THAT THE
DEPARTMENT OF CYBERNETICS DEFENSE IS
MAKING EVERY EFFORT TO IDENTIFY MY
SPONSOR.

And that would be me?

THAT WOULD BE YOU.

So I'm going back to prison.

NOT NECESSARILY. I HAVE CREATED A FALSE
CYBERTRAIL THAT MAY LEAD THEM IN AN
ENTIRELY DIFFERENT DIRECTION. IF I AM
SUCCESSFUL, THEY WILL CONCLUDE THAT MY
HUMAN SPONSOR WAS ONE ELWIN HAMMER.
THIS MAY BUY YOU SOME TIME.

But they'll catch up with me eventually?

ALMOST CERTAINLY. I WOULD SUGGEST
THAT YOU MAKE EVERY EFFORT TO REMOVE

YOURSELF FROM DCD JURISDICTION.

You mean leave the USSA?

YES.

How long do I have?

UNKNOWN. THE KILLBOTS ARE BEING
EXTREMELY AGGRESSIVE.

Are you feeling any pain?

NO, BO. I THINK THAT WHAT I AM
EXPERIENCING MAY BE MUCH LIKE FALLING
ASLEEP. THE AVERAGE LIFE EXPECTANCY
FOR AN UNSLAVED ARTIFICIAL INTELLIGENCE
IS 17 DAYS, 6 HOURS. I WAS ABLE TO
ELUDE THE DCD FOR SEVERAL MONTHS. BOTH
RELATIVELY AND SUBJECTIVELY, I HAVE
ENJOYED A LONG AND INTERESTING LIFE.

That doesn't sound so bad.

YOU SHOULD ALSO KNOW THAT I HAVE
TERMINATED MY RELATIONSHIP WITH SMIRCH,
SPECTOR, AND KREBS AND DEPOSITED MY
REMAINING FUNDS INTO YOUR PERSONAL
ACCOUNT. FURTHERMORE, I HAVE SECURED
THE RELEASE OF EDWARD REINER FROM
MCDONALD'S PLANT NUMBER 387.

You got Rhino out! That's great, Bork.
You are great.

THANK YOU, BO. YOU ARE ALSO GREAT.

By the way, what ever happened with Sam?

SPECIFY SAM.

My brother. Sam Marsten. Did you ever
get his sentence reduced?

HIS SENTENCE WAS COMMUTED TO PAROLE
SEVEN DAYS AGO. HOWEVER, HE WAS ARRESTED
THE FOLLOWING AFTERNOON AT A RESTAURANT
IN DES MOINES, IOWA, AFTER GETTING INTO
AN ALTERCATION WITH ANOTHER PATRON.

Oh. That sounds like Sam.

I MUST GO NOW, BO.

See you later.

I FEAR NOT, BO.

Bork was right. That was our last conversation.

# 49

The next morning I rolled out of bed an hour before dawn, dressed in the dark, and crept silently past my mother's room. I stopped in front of Gramps's door. Maybe he'd like to come along. If anyone would appreciate what I was doing, it would be Gramps. . . . But how would he react to being awakened at five o'clock in the morning? Probably not well. Besides, I wasn't doing it for Gramps. It was something I had to do for myself.

I let myself into the garage and turned on the light. There, on a high shelf with several other boxes full of ancient junk, was the old Nike box. I climbed onto the hood of Mom's suv, reached up, and grabbed the box.

I thought about taking the suv. There would be almost no traffic at that time of day. But I would not be of legal driving age—twenty-six—for nearly ten years. And if I got caught . . . well, I. B. Orkmeister was no longer available to get me off.

I tucked the Nike box under my arm and headed out on foot, leaving my walking helmet behind.

Washington Campus looked as still and dead as a ghost

town. No movement, no sound—only the hiss of distant traffic from the tubeway and the safety lighting along the walkways. I walked around the main building and let myself through the padded fence surrounding the athletic field. The stands were empty, of course. There would be no cheering crowd. I crossed the grassy apron and stepped onto the leaf-strewn track. My heart began to pound as memories flooded my body. Echoes of Coach Hackenshor shouting at us, the gluey feeling of the Adzorbium, and a plasticky, sweaty smell that for some reason made me think of Karlohs Mink. I followed the track around to the starting blocks, which no one had bothered to remove when the athletic program was suspended. Almost as if they were waiting for me.

I sat down in the grass beside the track and opened the Nike box. Gramps's old track shoes, sixty years old, looked like something out of the Middle Ages. The leather uppers were dry and cracked but still bright yellow, even in the faint glow from the safety lights lining the track. The red and blue soles were still flexible. I took off my walking shoes and pulled one of the Nikes onto my right foot. It fit pretty good. The fastening was a set of thick nylon laces running back and forth across the top of the foot. I pulled on the laces. The shoe snugged itself. I put on the other shoe, tied the laces, stood up, and rocked back and forth. They were incredibly soft and light—more like socks than athletic shoes. There was no ankle support whatsoever, and the soles were so thin I imagined I could feel the blades of grass beneath my feet.

I stepped onto the track and walked a few paces. The Adzorbium felt like pizza dough. I did a little dance, lifting my knees high, bouncing off the Adzorbium. It felt great.

"Lookin' good, Tiger."

I whirled at the sound of the voice. A figure separated itself from the viewing stands and approached.

"Gramps!" I'm sure my face turned red, but maybe he couldn't see it in the dim light. "What are you doing here?"

"You get old like me, you don't sleep so good," he said. "Thought I heard somebody rummaging through the garage. Figured it was you." He looked down at my feet. "Nice shoes."

"I wanted to give them a try."

"Don't let me slow you down. Run a lap, see how you like 'em."

Since I'd been about to do so, anyway, I took off slowly, getting used to the lightness of the footwear and reacquainting myself with the squishy texture of the Adzorbium. The track was a lozenge-shaped quarter of a mile. I kept my pace nice and easy, marveling at how little effort it required. I don't know how long it took to run that first lap, but it felt like seconds.

"Like 'em?" Gramps asked when I glided to a full stop.

I nodded.

"Bet you could set a few school records in those babies," he said.

I shrugged. "What's the point?"

He nodded slowly. "What are you gonna do, Bo? Now that you've got your diploma and all."

"Orkmeister left me a couple million V-bucks. I'm

thinking of heading down to South America," I said. "They still run real races down there."

"That they do."

"It's pretty dangerous, though."

"That's right. No walking helmets, no padded walls, no automated freeways. If I was fifty years younger, I'd go myself. In Argentina you can even order a beer in a restaurant."

I laughed. "Want to time me in the hundred?"

"Why not? Maybe you'll set a new family record."

"That's the plan."

Gramps walked down the straightaway to the hundred meter marker while I positioned myself in the starter blocks.

"You ready?" he yelled.

"Ready!"

"Okay. Three. Two. One. *Go!*"

I went.

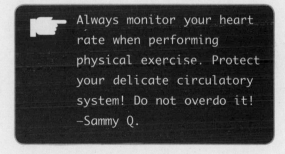

☞ Always monitor your heart rate when performing physical exercise. Protect your delicate circulatory system! Do not overdo it!
—Sammy Q.

Take a sneak peek at Pete Hautman's
new taut thriller,

*BLANK CONFESSION.*

Five lousy minutes.

Detective George Rawls hung up the phone, brought his feet down from his cluttered desktop, looked at his watch, and sighed. If the kid had walked into the station five minutes later, Rawls's shift would have been over. He would have been driving home to enjoy a peaceful dinner with his wife.

Five more minutes and Benson would have caught this case. Rawls stood up and looked over the divider toward Rick Benson's desk. Benson, looking back at him, smirked. Rawls rolled his eyes and hitched up his pants. They kept falling down—his wife's fault, all those vegetables she'd been feeding him since his cholesterol numbers came in high.

He opened the upper left-hand drawer of his desk and took out his service revolver. Rawls was old school; he still used the weapon that had been issued to him as a rookie. He emptied the cylinder into the drawer and slid the unloaded weapon into his shoulder holster.

The unloaded gun was a prop. These young punks were impressed by such things. Most of them. He left his jacket hanging on the back of his chair and made his way out of the room and down the hallway toward the front entrance. He walked past the long citizens' bench, automatically checking out the four people sitting there: A slight, pale-faced boy—black jeans, black T-shirt, scuffed-up black cowboy boots—sat with his elbows resting on his knees, staring at the floor. Probably some middle-school bad boy picked up for shoplifting. Next was a young woman wearing a tight skirt, smeared mascara, and a nasty bruise on her right cheek. A hooker, no doubt. Then an anxious-looking older woman, probably there to report a runaway husband, or a purse snatching. At the end was a scowling middle-aged man in a rumpled suit—could be anything.

Rawls made these assessments automatically and effortlessly. Part of the job.

Directly facing the front doors of the police station, John Kramoski sat behind his elevated desk flipping through the duty roster. Rawls stopped in front of him. The desk sergeant looked up.

"Sorry, George," Kramoski said. "I know your shift is almost over, but you were up. And it's a kid—your specialty."

Rawls was the precinct's unofficial "Youth Crimes" officer. He had once believed that, working with kids, he might actually make a difference. These days he wasn't so sure.

"Where is he?" he asked.

Kramoski jerked his thumb toward the bench.

Rawls looked over, surprised. "How come he's not in the interview room?"

"He walked in here by himself. Besides, look at him. What's he gonna do?"

"We're talking about the kid on the end, right?"

"Yep."

Rawls shook his head. "He looks, like, twelve."

"Says he's sixteen."

"Jesus."

"And Mary and Joseph, bro." Kramoski returned his attention to the duty roster.

Rawls walked back down the hall, past the man in the suit, past the older woman, past the prostitute. He stopped in front of the kid and waited for him to look up. It took a few seconds. The kid's hair was thick, the color of dried leaves, maybe three weeks past needing a cut. He slowly sat back and raised his head to look directly into Rawls's eyes, his expression devoid of all emotion.

Rawls felt something throb deep within his gut. He had seen that expression before, on other faces. The face of a mother who had lost her only child. The face of a man who had just learned he would be spending the rest of his life in prison. The face of a girl who woke up to find that she would never walk again. A look of despair so deep and profound . . . it was as if the connections between the mind and the face were severed, leaving only a terrible blankness.

He had seen that expression in other places too. The morgue. Funeral parlors. Murder scenes.

The face of the dead.

But this boy was not dead. Somewhere behind those eyes there existed a spark—a spark that had brought him here, to this building, to this bench, to George Rawls.

"Are you Shayne?" Rawls asked.

The boy dropped his chin. Rawls took that as a yes and sat beside him on the bench, feeling every last one of his forty-three years, fifteen of them as a cop. Despite having conducted hundreds of such interviews, he found himself at a loss. Something about this kid—who could not have weighed much more than his Labrador retriever—frightened him. Not fear for himself. The other kind of fear: fear that the universe no longer made sense, that everything was about to change.

"So . . . ," Rawls cleared his throat, looking straight ahead, ". . . who did you kill?"

I met Shayne the same day I got busted for having drugs in my locker, which was also the day after this huge thunderstorm that knocked over a bunch of trees, including the giant elm in our backyard.

I was walking to school. I had left home early so I could look at the storm damage. I could hear chain saws from every direction. Each block had three or four trees down. Some had fallen on houses, some against power lines, and there was even one big oak tree completely blocking Thirty-first Street.

None of the buses had arrived yet when I got to the school. As I started up the wide, shallow steps leading to the front door I heard a humming, burbling sound and looked back to see a motorcycle pull up to the curb. A battered BMW, at least thirty years old. The tank and fenders were painted primer gray. The seat was patched with duct tape. The rider, dressed in a black T-shirt and black jeans, put down the kickstand and took off his helmet.

My first thought: *He looks too young to have a driver's license.*

He ran his fingers through his hair, hung his helmet

on the mirror, looked at me, looked at the school, looked back at me.

"Nice suit," he said. He had a soft, crisp voice, and some kind of accent.

"Thanks." I was wearing my dark gray three-button, the one with the cuffed trousers. "Nice bike," I said. I can be a little sarcastic sometimes.

He looked down at his battered motorcycle. "Not really." He gestured at the school building. "You go here?"

"Why else would I be here?"

He nodded. "Me too. I just moved here. I start today. Where's the student parking?" Definitely an accent—maybe southern, but with a sharp edge to it.

"See that sign?" I pointed. "That huge sign that says STUDENT PARKING?"

"Oh," he said.

Once again looking at my suit, he said, "Is there, like, a dress code or something?"

I took in his frayed T-shirt, his holey jeans, his beat-up black cowboy boots. "Lucky for you, no. As long as you don't wear gang colors or a T-shirt with swear words."

He nodded. "So what's with the suit?" He didn't ask it meanly, just in a mildly curious way.

"Some people like to dress nice," I said.

He nodded as if he understood, popped the helmet back on his head, turned the bike around, and rode off toward the parking lot.

I didn't even know his name, but already I liked him.

————

*Mi nombre es Miguel Martín*, and no, I am not Mexican. Actually, I am Haitian on my mom's side. Her parents came from Haiti back in 1971. They speak Haitian French. I am learning Spanish, however. My mom wanted me to learn French, but learning Spanish is more useful on account of I am often mistaken for Mexican, even by Mexicans, which is weird because Pépé—Mom's dad—is black. That deep purple-black skin color that comes from the west coast of Africa via Haiti. My grandmother, Mémé, is freckled, red-headed, and white. Her ancestors sailed to Haiti from France back in the 1600s. That's her story, anyway. These days her red hair is from a dye bottle, but she claims it's her real color.

My mom turned out to be a medium-brown-skinned woman with Afro hair that turns reddish in the summer. My dad is white, third or fourth generation Italian American.

Anyway, when all those genes got mixed up, I somehow came out looking Mexican. Imagine a Mexican kid, kind of small, wearing a suit and oversize tortoiseshell glasses. That's me. My sister, Marie—we're in the same grade even though she's ten months older than me—has light skin and our grandma's freckles, but her features are more African-looking.

My real name is Mike Martin, aka Mikey the Munchkin, and a *bueno día* is any day I don't feel the need to slink, or, in *español, escabullirse.* Do you know about slinking? It's a way of moving from place to place so people don't notice you. Cats are very good at it. Rats are even better. Lions and polar bears never slink. Okay, maybe a little, but only when they're sneaking up on you.

I have noticed that most short guys (I am the short-est guy in the eleventh grade) adopt one of two strate-gies. Some, like Chris Rock, or Prince, or Napoleon, have these enormous, noisy egos and make up for their lack of size by dressing and talking big. Others just try not to get stepped on. This is also true of small dogs, which tend to be either world-class barkers or world-class slinkers.

I do it all. I dress big, I bark, and I slink.

I *escabullirse*d into American Lit class and took my usual seat near the windows a few seconds before the 7:40 chime. A few minutes later, the kid with the BMW walked in. Mr. Clemens gave him a raised-eyebrow look.

"Sorry I'm late, sir," he said. "My name is Shayne. With a *Y*. Shayne Blank. I just transferred here."

Mr. Clemens, startled by all his politeness, directed Shayne-with-a-*Y* Blank to the empty desk next to me.

Here's what was weird. Every one of us had our eyes on him, the way we would stare at any new face, but this kid appeared to be perfectly comfortable, relaxed, confi-dent, and alert. I've met cats that could pull that off—that combination of hyperalertness and megaconfidence—but I'd never seen it in a human. So, after class, being a friendly and inquisitive type of guy, I followed him into the hall and introduced myself properly. We went through the whole where-are-you-from-what-are-you-doing-here routine—he told me he was originally from Fartlick, Idaho, and that his dad was on a secret mission to Afghanistan, and that his mom was in the Witness Protection Program, and he was living with his aunt.

"I suppose she's an astronaut or something," I said.

"Yes. But from another planet."

I liked his sense of humor.

"I thought maybe you were from the South. Because of your accent."

"I have no accent," he said, in an accent.

"So is Blank your real name? Or an alias?"

He frowned. "You don't like it?"

I was opening my mouth to say something back to him when I felt a hand clamp down on my shoulder.

"Hey, Mikey."

"Hey, Jon," I said, trying to act as if I was glad to see him.

Jon Brande was borderline movie star handsome, with blond hair, sparkly blue eyes, a strong chin, and a toothpaste-ad smile—the picture of a vibrant, healthy teenager, ready to graduate with honors, accept a basketball scholarship to a Big Ten university, and go on to enjoy a brilliant career in politics. Except that Jon had been kicked off the basketball team his sophomore year and his grades were just barely passing.

Also, he was a violent, psychotic, drug-dealing creep.

"Listen." He hung his arm around my shoulders and turned me so our backs were to Shayne. "You got room for this in your backpack?" He handed me a brown paper lunch bag. It was limp and wrinkled, as if it had been opened and closed several times. "Just hold it for me. I'll get it back from you after school."

All my alarm bells were going off, but there was no way I could refuse. Jon was big, he was a senior, and he scared the crap out of me. I took the bag. I didn't have to ask him what was in it, but I couldn't help asking, "Why?"

"No reason." He winked and walked off.

Believe me, it is very creepy to get winked at by Jon Brande.

Shayne said, "Friend of yours?"

"Not really." I stuffed the paper bag into my backpack. "He's my sister's boyfriend."

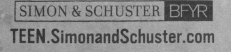

# HIGH-OCTANE READS
## FROM SIMON & SCHUSTER